Rank 6:
Firestorm

pe

Rank 6:
Firestorm

Barry McDivitt

thistledown press

Thistledown Press Ltd.
410 2nd Avenue North
Saskatoon, Saskatchewan, S7K 2C3
www.thistledownpress.com

Library and Archives Canada Cataloguing in Publication
McDivitt, Barry, 1953–, author
Rank 6 : firestorm / Barry McDivitt.
Issued in print and electronic formats.
ISBN 978-1-77187-162-4 (softcover).–ISBN 978-1-77187-163-1
(HTML).–ISBN 978-1-77187-164-8 (PDF)
I. Title. II. Title: Rank six.
PS8625.D59R36 2018   jC813'.6   C2018-904561-2
C2018-904562-0

Cover and book design by Jackie Forrie
Printed and bound in Canada

Canada Council Conseil des Arts
for the Arts du Canada

SASKATCHEWAN ARTS BOARD | cultivating the arts

Thistledown Press gratefully acknowledges the financial assistance of the Canada Council for the Arts, the Saskatchewan Arts Board, and the Government of Canada for its publishing program.

ACKNOWLEDGEMENTS

I'm not certain how many forest fires I covered during a thirty-year career as a journalist, but it is probably around 200. Sadly, many friends and acquaintances have lost their homes and almost everything they own to wildfires. On several occasions, while I was covering a fire, the winds suddenly picked up or changed directions and new fires broke out all around. I'd have to beat a hasty retreat and hope the only access road was still open. Generally I would look for an escape route while the Global TV cameramen I was working with would steadfastly shoot video until the last possible moment. I particularly remember the dedication of photographers Steve Beskidny, Jim Douglas and Chris Sobon.

Of all the government agencies I ever dealt with, at the provincial or federal level, the one that impressed me the most is the British Columbia Wildfire Service. It is internationally recognized as a leader in wildfire management and has some of the most dedicated men and women I have ever met. Every time I went to a fire zone I'd see sweat-drenched, soot-covered firefighters doing everything in their power to save lives and property. At a time when getting even routine information out of government agencies was becoming increasingly difficult, the BC Wildfire Service did everything in its power to make sure the public was kept informed. I was never turned down when I asked for information or an interview.

I'd like to thank Thistledown for continuing to show faith in me and my editor Harriet Richards for her excellent advice and guidance.

For my wife Alison —
because a good muse is hard to find.

One

This is what it will look like when the world ends.

The thought came suddenly to Emily. Once she would have found it disturbing. Now it was oddly thrilling. For a moment she considered sharing it with the others. Emily glanced around the van. There was tension on every face, except for a cheerful boy with Down syndrome. Emily suspected the boy didn't even realize everyone else was spooked. He appeared to be about thirteen, two or three years younger than Emily and the other campers.

She was the calmest person in the vehicle, a situation that would have amazed anyone who knew her well. Even Big John, the expedition leader, was finding it hard to keep his composure. He was middle-aged, imposingly tall and broad shouldered. His company brochure described him as ex-military and an expert on wilderness survival. Earlier that morning, at the meet-and-greet in a parking lot, he'd never stopped smiling. Emily thought it was unnatural, even a little creepy Now the smile was gone. He was driving the van and finding it difficult to see through the haze.

Emily decided not to say anything about the impending apocalypse. Nobody would want to hear her opinion. They never did. She knew perfectly well that she was a loser, but at least she'd always been considerate of the feelings of others. No point in making anyone else feel worse than they already were.

The van was large enough to hold nine campers and all their gear. Emily sat in the middle of the first passenger bench. The rear-view mirror was directly in front of her. She made the mistake of looking up and seeing her reflection. Emily shuddered and looked away. Her hair was half-curl and half-frizz at the best of times. It was also, as she'd been told by a classmate on the last day of school, an unusually unattractive shade of red. That morning her hair was especially unruly. Her face, already home to a galaxy of freckles, was scientific proof that not all acne medications are effective.

Being in the middle seat sucked. People you don't know, and don't want to know, on either side of you. Not even a window to yourself. Not that there was much to see anyway. The smoke was so thick you couldn't tell if you were passing houses, farms, or forest. Sitting to Emily's right was a pretty blonde girl who appeared to be addicted to technology. Big John had taken away her phone and tablet, but her fingers and thumbs never stopped moving. It was as if her hands were playing a game on an invisible touch screen. It was irritating.

Emily and the tech addict were the only two girls on the trip. They hadn't exchanged a word and had barely looked at each other. Neither one of them wanted to be there. Emily, normally desperate to fit in, stared at her lap. She'd paid so little attention to her surroundings and companions that she didn't even know for sure how many other teens there were or what most of them looked like.

The camper sitting to her left, a boy with a Jamaican accent, was squirming uncomfortably in his seat. Emily assumed he was just stretching. Her own legs, which she considered unnaturally long, were also starting to cramp. But it wasn't his legs that were bothering the boy. He took an inhaler out of a jacket pocket and began sucking at it in desperation. Emily looked at him with concern, nearly asked if she could help, but caught herself in time and lowered her head once again. The foul air was obviously affecting him badly.

Big John momentarily took his eyes off the road and turned to the boy. He watched with concern as the youngster wheezed. "You gonna be okay?"

Although tears were streaming from the boy's eyes he tried to smile and began to cough.

For some reason the coughing fit stimulated conversation. Emily closed her eyes, hoping to be ignored.

A thin voice from the back said, "I heard that most of this smoke came all the way from California."

"The fires seem to be getting worse every year," said a different boy.

"This is one of the driest summers I can remember," said Big John. He wiped the inside of the windshield with a huge hand, as if that was going to improve visibility. "I heard there are more than forty fires burning in the province right now. Luckily there aren't any in this region."

Big John was driving slowly because the smoke was so thick he could only see a few metres ahead.

"What's that fuzzy red ball?" Emily recognized the voice of the Down syndrome boy.

"That's the sun, Todd," said Big John. "The smoke makes it look that way."

"Did you guys know that fire is the only thing that goes up a hill faster than it comes down?" Emily had no idea who said it, but nobody seemed to care enough to challenge the statement or to agree with it.

The van felt like it was moving at about the same speed as an elderly person walking their dog.

An angry voice asked, "Why are we still doing this? It's obviously not safe to go into the bush right now. We can't even light a campfire because there's a fire ban."

"That's all true," said Big John. He was finding it increasingly difficult to sound cheery. "But it doesn't mean we can't have a fun and educational camping experience. We're going to spend the weekend at a private campground."

The van was filled with groans and curses. There was a single cheer, from Todd, the kid with Down syndrome. Under normal circumstances Emily would have made a point of talking to Todd and making sure he felt included. However, there no longer seemed any point to being inclusive.

"We're supposed to go wilderness camping," complained a boy. It was a voice Emily hadn't heard before. "Now you tell us we're going to a commercial campground. It sounds like the sort of place where my grandparents go with their RV."

Big John was getting annoyed. "As it was pointed out, correctly, a few minutes ago, it isn't safe to take you into the forest right now. This campground is the next best thing."

The complainer's voice now shook with anger. "You just don't want to give any refunds. I demand that you turn around and take us home."

Emily's opened her eyes in alarm. Everything would be ruined if the trip was cancelled.

Luckily Big John wasn't about to back down. "You may have had the opportunity to go camping before, but some of these other kids haven't."

The bickering went on for a while longer, but Emily didn't pay any attention. Restless, she fiddled with the old blue fanny pack she'd found in the basement. It had probably belonged to her father, who had zero fashion sense. Fanny packs were completely out of style and nobody, except for tacky tourists, wore them anymore. Emily had grabbed it because it was the perfect size to hold the rope.

She unzipped the pack and reached inside to run her fingers along the nylon rope she'd bought on sale at the dollar store.

"What's that?" Big John had heard the zipper and took his eyes off the road long enough to glare at Emily. Kids were always trying to smuggle their phones and other electronic devices into the bush, even though it was forbidden. He didn't want campers sending texts or playing games when they were supposed to learn how to start a fire by rubbing two sticks together.

"It's just some rope," said Emily, meekly. Surely he wasn't going to confiscate it. Her two seatmates turned to look at her.

"Pass it up," ordered Big John. He'd brought the van to a full stop. She complied with the order.

"Why did you bring rope?" he asked. Emily sensed that his suspicion had been replaced by simple curiosity. Although she couldn't immediately think of a logical reply, somebody else could.

"Rope is one of the most useful survival tools." It was the same know-it-all who'd said fire went uphill faster than it went down.

"That's what I read on an internet survival site," lied Emily. "I found the rope in our basement and I thought I'd bring it along, just in case."

Big John nodded. "I provide all the gear that we'll really need. But I don't mind if a camper brings along a few things like a magnesium fire starter or some rope. I don't let them bring knives. Not anymore." He frowned, as if remembering something very unpleasant. "Now, everybody shut up and pay attention. I'm pretty sure we're almost at the campground. I want everybody to keep their eyes peeled for a big sign that says Beaver Creek Campground. It'll be on the right hand side of the road." The vehicle started moving again. Slowly.

Emily couldn't see anything through the haze, but she pretended to look for the sign anyway.

"There it is!" Big John sounded relieved. He turned the van onto a bumpy dirt road.

Todd shouted, excited, "I can see fire."

"That's just the sun again," snarled the guy who'd demanded a refund.

"It looks like fire," insisted Todd.

"Yes, it looks like fire. I'm staring right at it. It's the sun!"

Over the next couple of minutes they passed several RVs heading the other way.

"People are leaving." It was the first time the girl sitting next to Emily had spoken.

"That's exactly what we should be doing!" It was the same jerk who had just barked at Todd. Emily snuck a peak and saw a tough-looking boy with a nose ring. Emily decided that she didn't like him, even though he was making some good points. "Nobody in their right mind wants to be here."

He was right. Everyone knew it. Except, apparently, Big John.

Two

Big John parked in front of a small, shabby building. A sign over the door identified it as The Office. "This is the office," he said, needlessly, and got out of the van.

As soon as he was gone the complaints began.

"This is stupid!"

"I'm supposed to be building character by roughing it in the wild. My probation officer isn't going to accept this."

"My parents said I needed to get more fresh air." The comment was followed by a dramatic and totally fake coughing fit.

Emily was the only one who didn't say anything. She was on the expedition because her father, who had recently left her mother and was starting a new family, was friends with Big John. The trip was supposed to be a present for Emily, although she couldn't think of anything she wanted to do less. Her father was probably getting it for free or at a huge discount.

Emily noticed that her rope had been left unattended on the driver's seat. As casually as she could she leaned forward and picked it up. If anyone noticed they didn't care. It went back into the fanny pack.

Big John returned from the office. "We're in luck. They only have one camping space left, but it's a big one. There's lots of room for us to put up our tents." He tried to smile, but couldn't pull it off. The trip had already turned into a disaster.

They drove for about ten seconds and stopped in a treeless, hard-packed strip of dirt next to the road. A sign said Overflow Parking. A rickety picnic table and rusted garbage barrel indicated the site was occasionally used for something other than parking.

"This is nice," someone muttered sarcastically.

"It's all they had left," snapped Big John. "They're booked up because of the long weekend."

"If we wait just a few more minutes there should be plenty of room," said the kid who was on probation. "It looks like lots of people are leaving."

He was right. A big pickup truck pulling a fifth-wheel drove by. Some campers had decided to pull out early.

"Those RV sites are too small for us," said Big John. "We have a lot of gear. Now, everybody out of the van."

For a moment it looked like Mr. Nose-Ring was going to refuse to leave the vehicle, but the expression on Big John's face made it clear he wasn't in the mood for drama. "We'll take a few minutes and stretch our legs. Then we'll set up the tents. Leave your bags in the van for now." He took out his cell phone and got back in the vehicle to make a call.

The other campers were forming a bond. Emily looked up just long enough to see there were eight of them. They crowded around the picnic table to bitch about their leader and speculate about who he was phoning.

Nobody noticed Emily stalk off. She wasn't in the mood to listen to complaints. The day had suddenly turned windy, kicking up dust and making the barren field even less appealing. It was hard to imagine a less appropriate place to experience wilderness camping.

Although many people were in the process of leaving, the campground was still a busy place. There were too many people for Emily's liking. It would be hard to find the privacy she needed.

An enormous and obviously expensive RV was parked nearby. The owners were folding lawn chairs and leaning them against the back of the vehicle. A trim grey-haired lady with kind eyes smiled at Emily. "We've decided to pack it in. My husband is having trouble breathing because of all the smoke. Besides, we find the heat oppressive. We're looking forward to air conditioning."

Her husband was bald and Emily noticed his sweat-shirt was too small to properly cover his bulging stomach. Water streamed from his eyes and he was clearly having difficulty catching his breath. "Normally we love camping, but this isn't fun at all," he said, opening an external storage compartment. "The only good thing about this smoke is that it's chased all the bugs away."

A small, white poodle came out of nowhere and charged Emily's ankles, barking furiously. It had a pink bow attached to the fur at the top of each ear.

"Stop it, Buttons!" The woman scooped up the poodle. "I'm sorry he startled you. Buttons always plays strange with people he doesn't know. Don't worry, he won't bite."

Buttons growled menacingly, as if trying to contradict his owner.

Emily wasn't fond of yappy dogs, but she generally got along with older people. Unlike the girls she knew from school they never told her that she was annoying, stupid and dressed wrong.

"I'm Anne Rossi," said the woman.

"And I'm Eric."

"Nice to meet you," said Emily, instinctively reverting to the good manners she normally possessed. "I'm Emily Morrisseau."

"I have a granddaughter named Emily," said Anne. "And our neighbours have a daughter named Emily. She's about your age."

"It's a common name," said Emily. The smile disappeared from her face. She'd been on a school trip where seven of the girls were named Emily. The other girls had given them nicknames, including Spicy Emily, British Emily, and Barbie Emily. She'd been Emily L. Because of her height, skinny frame, and long feet, her tormentors had decided that when she turned sideways she looked like the letter L.

Buttons had finally stopped barking, so Anne put him on the ground. The dog decided he didn't hate Emily after all. It pawed at her legs, demanding attention.

"You must still be in high school," said Anne.

"Yes, I'm just fifteen."

"Will you be missing your friends over the summer?"

Emily most definitely would not. She'd been voted Ugliest Girl in the School by the boys' soccer team. One of the worst days of her life was when she learned that a locker room conversation about female beauty had taken a cruel turn. Several girls who were seen as lacking in physical charm were nominated. There was a show of hands. Emily won. All the details were on Facebook. Everybody read it, which added to Emily's humiliation. The boys got in big trouble with the school. The ringleader was suspended.

Emily nearly answered with, "I don't really have any friends and I certainly don't like my school much," but decided that might lead to awkward questions. Instead she said, "I'm looking forward to some new experiences."

Eric peered into the smog. "Are you with that group of young people?" He began coughing.

"Yes. We're supposed to be on an outdoor adventure, where we learn all sorts of survival skills. It looks like this is as close as we're going to get to the wilderness. All the forest fires have messed things up."

Eric managed to catch his breath. "There's a man over there waving at you."

"That's Big John," sighed Emily. "He's our expedition leader. I'd better see what he wants. It was nice meeting you."

"He looks anxious," said Eric, peering through the haze. The wind picked up and a small dirt devil splattered the three of them with gravel.

Three

Just as Emily rejoined the other campers a rusty pickup truck with a Beaver Creek Campground logo on the door skidded to a halt in front of their picnic table. The driver rolled down the window and shouted at Big John.

"Don't unpack! A neighbour just called to say there's a fire burning on the other side of the highway. I'm going to check it out for myself." He sped off.

Todd was the only one who took the news calmly. "I told you guys I saw a fire," he said smugly. "Maybe now you'll listen to me."

"Everybody stay here!" shouted Big John. "Don't wander off." He quickly counted the campers to make certain nobody was missing. "Okay, I want everybody to get into the van in case we have to leave in a hurry."

"I think it's too late," said one of the boys. He pointed to the end of the access road, where a pine tree was burning. A large spark landed at his feet. He stepped on the ember and put it out.

"The fire has jumped the highway," said Big John. He was trying hard to speak calmly, although the sweat pouring off his forehead indicated his true feelings. "The wind is getting stronger every minute, and it's driving the flames. The access road will be closed shortly, if it isn't already."

Moments later his prediction came true. The campground pickup truck arrived in a cloud of dust. Emily suspected the driver must be the campground's owner. She thought the man looked and sounded like someone who had just realized that everyone he owned was about to be destroyed. His eyes bulged, sweat poured down his face, and his hands were shaking. "Get out right now!" he shouted. "Don't use the road. It's a death trap. Head toward the south end of the campground." He pointed to where he wanted them to go. "There's a path that runs along the creek. It will lead you to an iron bridge that crosses the highway. You'll be safe if you stay in the middle of the bridge." Then he drove off to shout the same warning to all the other campers.

Big John ran to the van and removed a backpack from under his seat. He handed it to the blonde girl, who appeared to be in a state of shock. "This has all the phones I confiscated from you guys. We'll need them to call for help or tell your parents that you're okay. Don't lose the bag. It's all we're taking."

The girl nodded, but fear had stolen her power of speech.

"Is everyone wearing proper footwear?" Big John took a quick look at their feet. Luckily nobody had removed their sturdy hiking boots. Emily's boots were a size too big. They'd belonged to her aunt, who had briefly dated an outdoorsman and bought the boots because she thought she'd have to go on lots of hikes. The relationship hadn't lasted and the aunt stored the boots in a closet until she discovered her niece was going camping. She'd been only too happy to give them away. The hiking boots felt heavy and awkward. Emily would have much preferred to be wearing light sports shoes.

The wide-eyed campers obediently fell in behind Big John, who led them to the campsite where Emily had met Eric and Anne Rossi. The elderly campers were each pulling a heavy suitcase behind them.

"Leave those behind," ordered Big John. "It's only stuff. You can easily replace possessions. Come with us. We have to get out of here."

His advice to the couple was sensible. They moved slowly, probably because of age, even after abandoning their luggage. They also seemed confused by the noise and smoke and Emily suspected they wouldn't make it very far on their own. The fire was moving too quickly. Anne was terrified and held Buttons tightly. The poodle was wild with fear and tried to squirm out of his owner's grasp. Eric offered to take the dog from his wife, but she realized he didn't have the strength to hold it. He was already gasping for breath and walking with difficulty.

The wind was becoming more intense with every minute. Red embers suddenly filled the air. It was like standing in a blizzard, but instead of snowflakes the campers were being pelted with hot coals. Sparks landed all around. Emily saw a clump of dried grass burst instantly into flames. She was astonished to see how quickly the fire was spreading. It made a terrible rushing sound, unlike anything she had ever heard before.

Trees lining the access road started to explode in the heat. Emily had no idea such a thing was even possible.

She stared, open-mouthed, as the trunk of a poplar tree was transformed into a cloud of splinters. The sound of the fire would have drowned out normal conversation, if anyone had wanted to talk. One of the boys suddenly screamed and started slapping his back. A large ember had landed on him, burning through his shirt and singeing the skin.

They joined a stream of people who were abandoning their campsites and vehicles. A few were carrying a handful of possessions, but most were leaving with nothing more than the clothes on their backs. Because the weather had been scorching hot for weeks, most of the campers weren't wearing more than shorts and T-shirts. Emily saw two teenage girls in bikinis and flip-flops. She was one of the few people who had covered her arms and legs. She was wearing jeans and a long-sleeved sweatshirt. It had nothing to do with modesty and everything to do with wanting to avoid insect bites, which always left her with ugly rashes and painful itches.

Emily was walking next to the Rossis, silently urging them to pick up the pace but recognizing that they were going as fast as they possibly could. They arrived a campsite where a middle-aged couple were having a furious fight. The woman wanted to join the campers fleeing on foot. Her husband wanted to drive their motorhome through the flames.

"It might ruin the paint job, but we'll make it."

Tears were streaming down her face. "We'll both die! Everything's on fire."

"The road isn't burning!" he shouted. "The road is made of dirt and dirt doesn't burn."

His rant was interrupted when a car parked near the campground office went up in flames.

The woman pointed toward the burning vehicle with a shaky hand. "That's what's going to happen to us if we try to drive out of here."

Her husband stared at the burning vehicle for a moment, turned pale, and grabbed his wife's hand. They looked around, unsure where to head, and finally noticed the column of refugees. Emily motioned for them to follow. At least her group had been given directions.

Big John's booming voice cut through the din. "There's no need to panic. If we look after each other we'll all make it."

There were quite a few older people and lots of families with kids. One woman was carrying a baby and trying to herd two other small children. Emily saw Big John scoop up the two youngsters and say something to the mother, who nodded and smiled weakly.

The refugees badly needed a leader and it looked to Emily that Big John was rising to the occasion. Earlier that day she'd been annoyed by what she considered his fake cheerfulness. Now she was impressed with how calm he was in a crisis.

Her fellow campers, who had been cursing their expedition leader just a few minutes earlier, now began to follow his example. They made sure nobody was in danger of being left behind, offering an arm whenever someone stumbled. A family had brought a parrot along on their camping trip and one of the boys was carrying the cage. Emily stayed next to Anne and Eric Rossi, who had been so friendly toward her. They were having trouble keeping up with the column and she felt protective of them.

The fire was moving toward them fast, jumping from one treetop to another.

Someone shouted, "There goes the campground offices."

Emily looked over her shoulder and saw flames shooting high into the sky. It was barely possible to see the outline of a building through the smoke. There was a loud explosion, followed by a second.

"There go the propane tanks!" said the man who'd been arguing with his wife.

"We're almost at the creek!" yelled Big John. "Hurry up! We've reached the trail."

There were already scattered fires on both sides of the trail. Emily could see it wouldn't be long before the small fires joined together to create solid walls of flame.

Anne tried to pick up the pace, but her foot hit a tree root and she stumbled. Buttons, who was still whining and wriggling, broke free from his owner's grasp. The poodle hit the ground hard, yelped, and raced toward an abandoned tent.

Anne screamed, "Buttons! Come here!"

The poodle seemed to have lost his mind. He barked hysterically as he ran behind the tent and out of sight.

The look of horror on Anne's face convinced Emily she had to act. She ran after the poodle, frantically calling his name. As she reached the abandoned campsite she saw the dog race behind a nearby tree.

"Emily! Come back! Leave the dog!" The voice belonged to Big John

Emily looked back toward the trail. Big John was still holding a child in each arm.

Anne and Eric Rossi clearly didn't want to leave their pet behind. They were being pushed and pulled along the path by some of the teen campers. Emily was just about to start running back toward the path when she heard a whine. Buttons stuck his head out from behind a tree. He was whimpering and shivering.

Trying to keep her voice calm Emily called the dog. The howling wind must have drowned out her voice. Buttons didn't seem to hear her. Emily called again, louder this time. The poodle heard and looked in her direction. Mustering all her self-control Emily walked steadily toward him, determined not to make any sudden moves that might spook it. She was almost within reach of the animal when they were engulfed by a cloud of sparks. Emily felt a searing pain on her left leg. A large ember had burned through the denim. She screamed and slapped at it. The spark dropped down the inside the pant leg, scorching flesh as it fell. Sobbing in pain and fear Emily turned to where she'd last seen Buttons. She was just in time to see it disappear into some thick bush.

"Buttons!" she yelled, knowing it was too late.

A powerful gust of searing wind knocked her to her knees. Emily got up, staggered a few steps, looked around, and was appalled to discover flames had nearly surrounded her. The way back to the path was blocked. She was alone.

A fearsome crackling above her head caused her to look up. The top of the tree she was standing under erupted in flame. All around, clumps of grass and small bushes were being set alight by the flying sparks. The smoke was suddenly so thick that the path to the creek was no longer visible. The roar of the fire was painfully intense.

Coughing from the smoke, swatting at the embers hurtling past her head, Emily turned and ran in the one direction where she could still see green. She had no idea where she was going or what lay ahead, but knew she only had seconds to escape.

The forest that surrounded the campground had very little underbrush, but the ground was covered with a thick carpet of dried needles and pine cones. An endless stream of flying embers was setting off a new fire every few seconds.

Emily pushed her way through a grove of saplings. The leaves were green, meaning they wouldn't flare up as easily as the pine needles. She paused, looking for an escape route and was dismayed to discover the blaze had encircled her. Emily had nearly given up hope when she noticed a huge log lying on the ground. The forest floor was burning in front of it, but the flames were only knee high. The log was acting as a fire break. Brush on the other side of the log wasn't yet burning.

Fuelled by terror she raced toward the fallen tree, hoping to hurdle the flames and land on top of the log. She wasn't a good jumper, and she sailed through, rather than over the blaze. Her feet landed on the log, but it was covered with slippery moss and she nearly fell backward into the fire. Recovering her balance at the last possible second, she lurched forward and then landed face-first on the hard ground. Winded, but knowing there wasn't a moment to spare, she got up and staggered into the unknown.

Four

Fighting to catch her breath Emily lurched from one tree to another, briefly holding on to each one for support. Her lungs burned from exertion and breathing in so much smoke. She frantically scanned the forest ahead. There was a slender strip of green, showing where the trees weren't yet aflame.

Spurred on by terror Emily began to run. At one point the fires on both sides were so close that it was like being in a hot oven. As she raced through the flames Emily found herself in a small clearing. The wind wasn't quite as strong as it had been a few minutes earlier, so she was able to put a little distance between herself and the flames.

She paused for a moment, trying to decide which direction to take, when she heard frantic voices and loud metallic banging. Emily turned toward the noise. The prospect of rescue gave her renewed strength. A dark shape bounded past, nearly knocking her over. It was a whitetail buck, galloping for its life. The deer had spent its entire life in this forest. Maybe it knew the way to safety. She ran after it and quickly found herself on a well-worn path.

The voices were clearer now. Two men were having a ferocious argument. One of them shouted, "Forget the boat!"

"No! I'm taking the boat!" yelled the other. "It will just take a minute."

"We don't have a minute!"

"Yes we do! I won't tie it to the trailer."

"That's pointless. It'll just fall off!"

Emily saw a flash of blue through the trees. A lake! Moments later she saw a wooden sign that read Hawkeye Lake Recreation Site. From her left came the sound of a car door slamming. Through the trees she caught a glimpse of an SUV with a boat trailer. There was an aluminum fishing skiff on the trailer.

"Don't go!" screamed Emily. "Wait for me! Please!"

The men couldn't hear her cry for help. It was drowned out by the roar of the fire. The wind had picked up again. The driver floored the accelerator and the SUV's wheels threw up a volley of stones as the vehicle sped away. The unsecured boat bounced wildly every time the trailer hit a rock or rut in the road.

The access road was flanked on both sides by sheets of flames, but the driver was clearly determined to race through them. Emily was nearly overcome with grief as she watched her ride to safety disappear. Moments later there was a thunderous crash. Emily assumed the boat had fallen off the trailer.

Sensing that the lake offered the only hope of escape Emily ran to the water's edge. The boat launch was just a muddy bank that gently sloped into the lake. There was an oar lying on the ground, next to a large cooler. A half-eaten lunch was spread across a nearby picnic table, proof that the forest fire had moved so quickly that people were caught off guard. Several fishing rods leaned against a tree.

The lake was long. She couldn't see either end. The opposite shore was far enough away that it would have been barely possible to see people walking on the shoreline. There were a number of cabins on the other side. A few were close together, but most sat alone on big lots, close to the water. Hopefully someone had decided to spend the long weekend at their cottage and would see her standing at the boat launch.

Emily wished the men had left the aluminum boat behind. She could have pushed it into the water and then use the oar to pole herself out into the lake and away from the rapidly approaching flames.

Nobody on the opposite shore was coming to rescue her. That was now obvious. Even if someone saw her they wouldn't be able to cross the lake in time. She was going to have to swim to safety. Swimming was one of the many athletic activities that Emily wasn't very good at, but at least she'd taken lessons as a little girl. She realized it would be impossible to swim with heavy hiking boots on her feet. She took the boots off, tied the laces together, and hung them around her neck.

The cooler that had been abandoned by the fishermen contained a bag of ice and half a dozen cans of beer. It was made of thick plastic and had a lid that locked securely into place. Even better, it had large carrying handles that would make it easier to hold on to. Emily tipped the cooler over, scattering ice and cans of beer across the ground. She locked the lid into place and tossed the container into the water. She was relieved to see that it bobbed on the surface. It should make an excellent float.

On the shore, near the oar, was a log. It was as thick as Emily's arm and nearly as long as she was. Somebody had probably put it there to use as firewood. By tucking the oar and driftwood under one arm, and holding onto the cooler with the other hand, she might have enough buoyancy to keep from drowning.

She'd just taken her first tentative step into the lake when, incredibly, Buttons came running down the same path that had led Emily to the lake. Somehow the poodle had managed to escape the inferno and find her. Perhaps it had heard her screaming after the SUV. Shaking and whining, looking like it was about to suffer a heart attack, it crouched at Emily's feet.

"This is all your fault!" raged Emily.

Buttons whimpered pathetically and cowered.

"What am I supposed to do with you?"

The girl and dog suddenly found themselves in the middle of another spark storm.

The wind was pushing the fire steadily closer. In a matter of seconds the heat became too intense to tolerate. Emily glanced over her shoulder and saw a cloud of ash coming straight toward her. She turned, felt hot air envelop her body, and staggered into the shallows. Buttons followed, determined to stay close to the only human in sight. The poodle had short legs and only managed to take a few steps into the water before he had to start swimming. Emily had risked her life back at the campground to save the dog and felt she couldn't leave the helpless animal behind now. She picked up Buttons and tossed the tiny,

shaking body into the cooler. Then she snapped the lid
shut and walked into deeper water.

The bottom was mushy. Emily felt a sharp jab at the
bottom of her right heel, causing her to yelp. Limping
slightly, she kept going until the water was nearly up to
her waist. Then she fell forward and felt the blessed chill
of the water.

Five

T he cooler floated well, even with Buttons inside. The poodle reacted violently to being imprisoned in a dark, airless box and scratched incessantly at the plastic sides. Holding onto the cooler with her right hand, and with the oar and log tucked under her left arm, Emily was able to keep her head above water. Fear surged through her body, giving her renewed strength. Furious kicking propelled her steadily away from shore and toward what she hoped was safety.

After several minutes, winded from her exertions and needing to catch her breath, she turned her head toward the boat launch to see how close the flames were. An ember immediately flew into her left eye. She shrieked and ducked her face into the lake to put it out. It was a painful lesson. She wasn't out of range of the fire just yet.

Emily started kicking again and quickly realized she was in serious trouble. The heavy hiking boots hanging from her neck had filled with water and the laces had twisted together. They were pulling her head under the surface and slowly strangling her at the same time. Reluctantly she let go of the cooler and used her free hand to untie the laces. The boots sank to the bottom.

The cooler floated high in the water, and it was caught by the wind once Emily released it. Although the oar and log provided some buoyancy, they probably weren't enough to get her safely to the far shore. She kicked furiously, knowing she had to reach the cooler while she still had the time and strength. Several times she was almost able to touch it when another gust of wind propelled it out of reach.

When she was finally able to grab one of the cooler's handles Emily was gasping for air. Her own shortness of breath reminded her that the poodle had a very limited supply of air inside the cooler. Buttons had suddenly gone quiet. Emily realized he would soon suffocate, if he hadn't already.

By tucking the oar under one armpit and the log under the other, Emily struggled to get stable enough in the water to unlock the lid. She finally succeeded, opened the cover a crack and was rewarded with a feeble bark. Buttons was still alive. He moaned pathetically. With the poodle's air supply replenished she closed the lid and resumed kicking. It wasn't long before sheer exhaustion forced her to stop. Luckily the strong winds helped push the cooler, with her hanging on for dear life. The visibility was getting steadily worse. As the smoke got thicker it became increasingly challenging for Emily to tell if she was even going in the right direction.

Fatigue made it hard for Emily to hold onto the handle. She stopped her awkward dog-paddle for a moment, opened her mouth to take in a lungful of air, and accidentally swallowed water. Coughing, she almost lost her grip on the cooler. Then she saw something that immediately raised her spirits. Salvation was finally in reach.

Emily realized she'd almost made it across the lake. The welcoming shoreline was untouched by fire. Through the haze she could see it was reassuringly green. She saw two cabins standing only a short distance apart. One was small and tucked into the trees. The other was much larger and had a detached boathouse. Emily decided to aim for the boathouse, which was almost dead ahead.

The small log she'd been using as a flotation device was partly rotten. The strain of holding up her body was too much for it. The top third of the log broke off and the remaining section wasn't big enough to help keep her head above water. She let go of the remaining chunk of wood.

It suddenly dawned on Emily that it had been some time since she'd last heard any noise from inside the cooler. Once again she was consumed with guilt at the thought of accidentally letting the dog suffocate. Worn out, she struggled with the lid's locking device, taking longer than usual to open it.

Up until then the poodle had cowered at the bottom of the cooler every time the lid opened a crack. That time, the moment he saw some daylight, Buttons moved to break free from his dark and airless prison.

His leap overturned the cooler and knocked the lid out of Emily's hands. While the dog thrashed wildly in the water Emily reached for the cooler. Too late. The wind had caught it. Frantic, she managed to grab the lid. If she held the oar in one hand and the lid in the other it might be enough to keep her afloat for another few minutes.

Buttons swam around her in a circle, making a pitiful gasping noise. The lid was wide and flat and didn't easily fit under an arm. As she struggled with it Emily realized it wasn't much smaller than some of the boogie boards she'd seen little kids use at the beach. It might even be made out of a similar material. She didn't have the strength to pull herself onto the lid with just one hand so she let go of the oar. The lid wasn't big and buoyant enough to keep her whole body afloat, but it was enough to keep head and shoulders out of the water.

Emily felt sharp claws digging into her back and tearing open her shirt and skin. Buttons had managed to climb onto her shoulders. Although he was a small dog it was enough extra weight to force her face into the water. Emily twisted her body and felt the dog let go.

Buttons reluctantly swam away from Emily. At first he set an erratic course. Then, perhaps smelling the nearby forest, he headed straight toward land.

An enormous head suddenly appeared out of the smoky fog, just to Emily's right. She stared in disbelief, too shocked to move. An ugly face, with huge nostrils and wide eyes, was almost close enough to touch. It was also moving toward shore. The creature saw Emily and grunted menacingly. They were on converging paths and if Emily hadn't stopped kicking they would have collided. Already in a state of panic her brain simply froze. She had no idea what was happening or what she was looking at.

The massive head cut cleanly through the water. A smaller animal followed in its wake. Emily finally understood that she'd nearly run into a cow moose and her calf. The moose were powerful swimmers and quickly reached the shore. They climbed onto dry land, just a few metres from where Buttons had landed. The dog, perhaps awed by the size of the moose, didn't move or make a peep. The cow and calf didn't stop. They raced toward the forest and disappeared from view.

With the last of her strength Emily managed to once again pull herself onto the cooler lid. It wasn't big enough to keep her afloat unless she kept kicking, and her strength was nearly gone. Then came the instantly recognizable sound of a dog shaking the water out of its fur.

Emily raised her head and saw the poodle waiting for her on a pebble beach. If a puny mutt could make it, so could she. She closed her eyes, held tightly to the lid, and kicked until her feet touched bottom. Emily stood up. She was in front of the boathouse, in chest-deep water. Overcome with relief and exhaustion she crawled up a wooden ramp and vomited.

Six

After wiping the puke from her mouth Emily rose unsteadily to her feet. "Hello!" she called. "Is anyone here?"

There was no response. Buttons watched her from the beach, breathing heavily.

The boathouse was large and solidly built. The ramp she was standing on led to a heavy-duty garage door that could be raised to bring boats in and out. A professionally painted No Trespassing sign covered most of the door. From where she was standing Emily could see three other signs warning people to stay off the property. One of them, nailed to a tree, featured the picture of a revolver and warned that the property was protected by a Colt .45. The property's owners clearly didn't want any uninvited guests. Another sign read: Trespassers will be shot. Survivors will be shot again.

"I could sure use some help," she yelled. "Please don't shoot!"

Hearing no response she took a step and felt a jolt of pain. It reminded her that she'd cut her heel, probably on a piece of broken glass or sharp rock, when she'd gone into the lake at the boat launch. Emily took another step, looked down, and saw a bloody footprint.

Paving stones had been used to make a walkway that ran from the boathouse to the cabin. There was a door at the back of the boathouse, next to a large window. The door was locked and there were bars on the window.

Emily turned her attention to the main building. It was an impressive two-storey log cabin with a porch on the front and solar panels on the roof. Whoever owned it clearly had money. They were also security conscious. Iron bars protected every window on the ground level.

Emily limped to the front porch, followed by Buttons. It was obvious nobody was home. There was a huge padlock on the front door, but she knocked anyway. There were two wicker chairs and a glass-top table on the porch. Thankful for the opportunity to sit down she collapsed into one of the chairs and then took a close look at her injured foot. The cut wasn't too deep and it didn't look like there was any glass or dirt in the wound.

Emily closed her eyes and took some deep breaths, astonished that she had survived. Then it occurred to her how ironic it was that she felt that way. When she opened her eyes she noticed that the poodle had jumped onto the other chair and was watching her with wide eyes. Then she saw something that made her heart jump. Under the table was a pair of men's flip-flops. They were much too big and cheaply made, but they were better than bare feet. She slipped them on and decided to walk around the cabin and see if there was anything else she could use.

There was another door and several more windows at the back of the cabin, but they were all shuttered or locked. The only thing left outside was a rake, but it didn't seem to be of any use. Emily suspected that everything she needed to survive was inside the cabin. There would be food, clothing, and probably a first aid kit.

"If Big John hadn't taken away my cell phone I could be calling my mother right now." She was speaking to Buttons, who now seemed determined to keep her in sight at all times. "Of course, being in the lake for so long probably would have wrecked it anyway. I don't have a waterproof case for it. Too expensive." Buttons whined in sympathy. "Besides, there probably isn't cell service this far from town."

Emily limped back to the front porch. She sat down in the wicker chair and tried to figure out what was happening on the other side of the lake. The thickening smoke made it hard to see exactly what was going on, although towers of flame clearly showed where the tallest trees were being consumed.

It was time to make a plan. Something wasn't making sense, although she couldn't immediately put her finger on what it was. Then it dawned on her that there was no sign of a road at the back of the cabin. There was only wilderness. Access to this side of the lake must be by boat only. Trying to reach safety by walking through the bush wasn't an attractive option, especially with an injured foot. Besides, she didn't have the faintest clue about which direction to head in.

Emily remembered that while swimming across the lake she'd seen another cottage on the lakeshore. It probably wasn't far away. She got off the chair and, followed by the little dog, went in search of the other cabin. It didn't take long to find a path that ran close to the lakeshore. The trail was very narrow and largely overgrown. It didn't look as though there was much foot traffic between the two properties.

After just a couple of minutes Emily arrived at the other cabin, a run-down, flimsy old shack built of particleboard and weathered lumber. Several battered lawn chairs were clustered around a fire pit. Behind the cabin was a tall stack of split firewood. Next to the wood pile a couple of crudely constructed sawhorses supported a canoe. It rested upside down and was covered with an ancient, moss covered tarp. Set back from the cabin, at the edge of the forest, was an outhouse. There was no driveway or road. Once again the only access was by boat.

The rickety door wasn't locked and easily swung open. Emily stepped cautiously inside, aware she was trespassing. The only sources of light were a couple of small windows with dirty glass. She blinked until her eyes because accustomed to the gloom.

There wasn't much to see. The interior of the cabin was a single room. It was small and cluttered with shabby furniture. Emily had seen better kitchen tables at the side of the road with a FREE sign attached to them. It came with four mismatched chairs. The largest piece of furniture was a stained and tattered couch that might have been rescued from a dump.

In the very middle of the room was an old-fashioned wood stove. Leaning against it was an axe. Like everything else in the cabin it had seen better days. The blade was rusty and the handle had a crack running lengthwise down it, and was held together with duct tape.

Three or four mattresses leaned against the back wall. There wasn't a proper bed anywhere, so Emily assumed the mattresses were simply tossed on the floor and used as beds.

Near the doorway was a kitchen countertop and some cabinets that looked like they'd been rescued from a demolition site. There was a tiny stainless steel sink, but no faucet. The owner likely hauled water from the lake. Wastewater from the sink drained directly into the ground underneath the cabin. On the counter next to the sink sat a container of liquid dish soap and a stained towel.

Emily opened the cabinets to see if anything useful had been left behind. In the first cupboard there were a couple of cans of condensed milk, an almost-empty jar of instant coffee, a tin of tuna, a small can of beans, and a few pieces of beef jerky in a resealable plastic bag. There was also an ancient transistor radio, the smallest flashlight she'd ever seen, and a handful of no-name batteries.

She was delighted to find a small first aid kit, the kind you buy at the drug store for a few dollars. Emily opened it hopefully. It looked as though it had been gradually emptied over the years. There wasn't anything left in it except for some Band-Aids. It wasn't much, but it was better than nothing. At least she'd be able to bandage her heel.

The second cabinet was filled with an assortment of pots, pans, mugs, glasses, and plates. Nothing matched.

There were two drawers, one on either side of the sink. There was nothing in the first except for some short emergency candles and a few books of matches. Emily scooped them out of the drawer and put them on the counter.

The second drawer contained a plastic cutlery tray filled with a hodgepodge of knives, forks, and spoons. On impulse she lifted up the tray to see if anything was hidden underneath. There was. A single key. She assumed the key was for the unlocked door and put it back in the hiding place.

Emily kept looking for a light switch. Eventually it dawned on her that if there wasn't a road on that side of the lake there wouldn't be any power lines either. The big log cabin next door had solar panels on its roof and might even have its own generator, but the owner of this shack clearly didn't have the money for those luxuries. There was a Coleman camping lantern on the table, but Emily had no idea how to light it.

A number of large nails had been pounded partway into a wall, obviously used to hang clothes. There was a battered red ball cap on one of the pegs. It featured the logo of a sports team that Emily didn't recognize. Hanging from one of the other nails was a long-sleeved camouflage jacket that was covered in sawdust and smelled of sweat.

Emily glanced at her watch, which had survived the swim across the lake, and was surprised to see it was only noon. A lot had happened in just a few hours. It was much cooler in the cabin than it was outside and her wet, clammy clothes were starting to make her feel a little chilly.

After grabbing the dish soap and first aid kit Emily went outside. It was blisteringly hot and she warmed up right away. Followed by Buttons, she carried one of the decrepit lawn chairs to the lake and put it in shallow water. Then she sat for a few minutes and watched the distant fire with a mixture of awe and dread. The smoke was getting thicker, if that was possible, but huge plumes of flame would suddenly flare up and then slowly die. Every now and then there was the sound of an aircraft flying overhead. Emily knew that if she couldn't see the plane the pilot couldn't see her.

She carefully washed her wound with the dish soap. It was the closest thing to an antiseptic in the cabin and she thought it was better than nothing. Then she took off her shirt, used it to dry the injured foot, and put a Band-Aid over the cut. Leaning back in the chair, wondering what to do next, she absentmindedly unzipped the fanny pack and began fiddling with the rope. Holding the cord in her hands jolted her back to reality.

"I can't believe I went through all this trouble to stay alive," she muttered angrily. Buttons woofed quietly. He was sitting on the beach watching Emily with somber eyes.

"I must have panicked," Emily continued, talking directly to the poodle. "Being burned alive is one of the most painful ways to die. I never wanted to go that way, so I guess it made sense for me to escape." She thought for a moment. "I've read that drowning is actually peaceful. At the end, anyway."

Buttons wagged his tail.

"It could have been a perfect ending," sighed Emily, wiping away a tear. "I was in the middle of a lake, for cripes sake. All I had to do was let go of the oar and the cooler. There's no way I'd have been able to swim much longer. I'd be at the bottom right now. Even if they ever did find my body people would assume I'd drowned while trying to get away from the fire."

Buttons barked happily, glad to be included in the conversation.

"Of course, you'd have suffocated in the cooler. That wouldn't have been fair to you. It would be a terrible way to go."

Emily took the plastic wrapper off the rope. "I guess I'm back to the original plan."

The smoke was stinging her eyes and making breathing difficult.

"I think we should go inside for a while."

The poodle barked in agreement.

Emily stood up and, using the chair as support, hopped to shore on her good foot. She didn't want to get the Band-Aid wet. Once on shore she put on the flip-flops. She took one last look at the lake and noticed the cooler had drifted to shore and was just a short distance away. It wasn't likely she'd have any further use for it, but Emily wasn't the sort of girl who left litter behind. She picked up the container and left it outside the cabin.

The indoor air quality wasn't great, although it was better than outside. The dirty windows hardly let in any light and it was too dim for Emily to find her way around the cabin without turning on the small flashlight. She was pleasantly surprised by how much light it gave off. Emily lit one of the emergency candles and set it on a chipped plate, so it wouldn't start a fire if it tipped over. Then she lit a second one and put it on top of the cast iron stove. Two flickering candles provided barely enough light for her to walk around the cabin without bumping into things.

Once again feeling chilled, Emily figured it was time to dry her clothes. She decided to take a section of her rope, tie it between two trees, and use it as a clothesline. It was so hot outside that, combined with a strong wind, her clothes would dry quickly.

She looked in the cutlery drawer for a knife to cut through the rope. There was one with a dull, serrated blade. It barely made a mark on the rope. Then she remembered that there was something better.

Emily picked up the rusty axe and headed out the door. Buttons, reluctant to let her out of sight, followed. Emily found two suitable trees, measured the rope, and hacked off a piece with the axe. She put up the clothesline and then draped her pants and shirt over it. For a moment she seriously considered adding her underwear to the line of drying laundry, but couldn't bring herself to do it. "I'm so shy I don't even like stripping down in front of a boy dog," she told Buttons. "Besides, what if the people who own this cabin suddenly arrive by boat and they find me naked?"

In the end she decided to leave her underwear on and let it dry on her skin.

"Are you hungry?"

Buttons seemed to understand the question and barked enthusiastically. They went back into the shack and Emily found a can opener in the cutlery drawer. She opened the tin of tuna and put it on the floor. Buttons immediately began wolfing it down. Emily thought about opening the can of beans for herself, but didn't have any appetite.

Suddenly overcome with fatigue she sat on the couch, which was more comfortable than it looked. A few minutes the later the poodle finished his meal, jumped onto the couch, and snuggled against Emily's leg.

"I know you didn't mean any harm, but you are the cause of all this trouble." Emily's voice was gentle. She was too tired to be angry. "If you hadn't run off everything would be okay right now."

As soon as the words left her mouth Emily knew she was talking nonsense. She had no idea if everyone else from the campground was safe. The fire had moved with amazing speed and it was possible the refugees had been cut off. Perhaps she was the only one who'd survived. How ironic would that be?

Buttons nuzzled Emily's hand.

"Yeah, now you want to be my buddy. You weren't very friendly when we first met." She laughed bitterly. "I can't really blame you for not liking me at first. Hardly anyone does. I haven't had a real friend since grade three."

The dog yawned and put his head on Emily's lap.

"The good thing about dogs is that they don't care if people are considered cool or not. I'm pretty sure you aren't bothered by the fact I was voted ugliest girl in my school." She began sobbing. "Don't worry. Before I go I'll make sure you're okay."

Emily cried for awhile and held the dog tight. Buttons gave her a wet kiss. Emily smiled through her tears. "I know you are trying to make me feel better." She sighed.

"I'm going to go crazy if I just sit here. Time to get up and do something."

She went outside and discovered her clothes were dry, so she put them on. Of course they smelled of smoke but so did everything else. This time Buttons didn't follow her outside. The small dog was exhausted and refused to move from the couch.

Seven

The sun was slowly sinking in the west, a crimson ball that Emily could barely see through the haze. If possible the smoke was even worse than it had been earlier in the day. The wind had almost completely died down. In one way that was good, because the fire didn't appear to be spreading as quickly. On the other hand, now there was nothing to blow away the smoke.

The fire on the other side of the lake didn't look quite as ferocious as it had earlier in the day. A lot of the trees and forest litter had already burned. Fortunately the lake had acted as a moat, protecting the far shore and its vacation homes from flying sparks.

As she stood near the shack wondering what to do next, Emily's eyes fell on the cooler. It looked new. She remembered that she'd left the lid on the shore near the boathouse. A good cooler, as long as it had a lid, could be left behind as thank-you gift for the people who had unintentionally provided her with shelter and supplies. She decided to get the lid.

The hazy light that had persisted all day was now fading rapidly. Emily carefully made her way along the path that linked the two properties. The lid was beside the boathouse, right where she'd left it.

Curious about what was inside the building, she shone her flashlight through the window. On the floor in front of the window was a Jet Ski. She could also make out a workbench with a few tools lying on it. It didn't look as though there was anything of immediate use, and since someone who will soon be dead doesn't need to worry about long-term planning, she shrugged and walked away.

Emily carried the lid back to the shack and leaned it against the cooler. Then she went into the cabin, where the two candles were still burning. Buttons opened his eyes, briefly wagged his tail in greeting, and went back to sleep.

Hunger was finally setting in. Emily opened the can of beans and started eating them cold with a spoon. The smell of food woke the poodle up. He jumped to the floor, sat at Emily's feet, and begged for something to eat. She wasn't sure if dogs were supposed to like beans, or even if it would make them sick, but decided to take a chance. She took a small bowl out of the cupboard and put some beans in it. Buttons scarfed the food down and greedily licked up all the tomato sauce.

While searching for dishes and cutlery Emily had redis-covered the old battery-powered radio. She was desperate for news about the forest fire and turned it on. To her surprise the radio worked, although she was only able to find a single station. Luckily the station was local and its programming that day was focused entirely on news about the forest fire.

She learned that the fire had amazed everyone with how fast it had spread. It was still growing, but not as quickly because the wind had died down. The announcer said it was lucky the fire had been stopped on one flank by Hawkeye Lake.

Emily listened intently to an interview with a provincial fire official who said his crews couldn't fight a wildfire at night for safety reasons. The exhausted firefighters would have to leave the front lines, giving them a much-needed break, and would resume the battle in the morning. Unfortunately the weather forecast for the night was not good. It called for gale-force winds that could spread a forest fire at an incredible rate. There was a real risk it could turn into a Rank 6 fire. Rank 6 was the highest category of forest fire; it indicated a dangerous and unpredictable inferno. There was also the risk of thunderstorms. Heavy rain would be welcome, but lightning strikes could start more fires and make the situation even worse.

The firefighting situation across the province was so desperate that other parts of the country were sending help. Alberta and Saskatchewan were sending as many trained fire crews as they could spare and five water bombers were on their way from Quebec.

The good news was that the Beaver Creek Campground had been successfully evacuated. The other campers had crossed the creek, made it to the safety of the iron bridge, were picked up by rescue crews, and driven to safety in school buses. The bad news was that a teenage girl was missing.

"At least your mom and dad are safe," said Emily, who was sitting on the couch beside Buttons. "I'm sure they are worried about you."

Emily thought about her own parents. By now they would have been informed that she was missing. They'd both be worried sick. Well, her mom for sure. Dad had never been terribly interested in her. The only reason Emily was on this stupid wilderness expedition was because he was feeling guilty for abandoning his family to start a new one. Also, he was probably getting the trip for free. It would never have occurred to her father to first ask Emily if she wanted to go camping. It angered Emily when she learned he'd booked the trip, and it was then she began to have dark thoughts. She wondered if anyone else had ever gone on a survival course, determined not to survive it.

Then Emily went numb. She heard Big John being interviewed on the radio. He was being called a hero because he'd successfully organized the campground evacuation and had personally carried two small children to safety. But it was obvious to anyone listening that Big John didn't feel like a hero. He considered himself a failure. One of the teenagers in his care was missing. He described how the girl had run directly into danger to save someone's dog. "It was the bravest thing I've ever seen in my life," sobbed Big John. "I just hope they're both okay."

Emily had never heard such intense pain in a person's voice. Although she hadn't meant to cause anyone grief, and chasing after Buttons had been done with the best of intentions, she realized Big John was sick with worry.

She turned off the radio and stretched out on the couch. Buttons climbed onto her lap. Emily was by nature a sympathetic person and couldn't rid herself of the suspicion that she'd just ruined Big John's life. He'd been responsible for her safety and, even though it wasn't his fault that she'd run after Buttons, he'd be blamed forever if people thought she'd died in the fire.

Emily made up her mind to look for a pen and paper in the morning so she could leave a note saying she and Buttons had survived the fire and she considered Big John a hero for helping to save all the other campers. She realized that it was highly unlikely that she was going to find any writing material. Emily closed her eyes, pulled the poodle onto her lap, and tried to figure out what to do next.

Eight

"I'm not sure how to do what I have to do and still keep you safe." Emily stroked the poodle's badly matted fur as she spoke. One of the pink ribbons was gone, but the other was still in place.

She absent-mindedly reached inside the fanny pack, which was again around her waist, and fingered the rope she was going to use to hang herself.

Emily could hardly remember a time when she felt happy and safe. Maybe when she was younger and people weren't so critical of her. Now, for some inexplicable reason, everything about her was wrong. Female class-mates were constantly criticizing her clothes and hairstyle. Some of the meaner girls called her stupid. She knew that wasn't accurate. Emily was actually very smart. She also worked hard at school and got good grades. And she was always respectful of others.

Now whenever Emily passed a mirror she studied her reflection carefully and wondered if she really was hideous. She had so many freckles that she'd convinced herself that her skin actually looked dirty. Having unruly carrot-coloured hair was definitely a curse. Her teeth were a little crooked because her parents couldn't afford braces, but nobody would notice unless she smiled. She rarely smiled anymore anyway. Certainly she would never make it as a model, although the kids who were cruelest to her at school definitely weren't much to look at either.

What was the point of living if every day brought fresh hurt and humiliation? Emily thought a lot about that question. On the day her father moved out she thought her heart had finally hit bottom. A few days later she discovered things could get even worse when she won the ugly girl contest. She started thinking about killing herself. For some reason the idea became more attractive every time she considered it. It promised an end to the pain.

Being sent on a wilderness survival expedition appeared to offer the perfect solution. She could slip away into the forest, find a sturdy tree branch, and hang herself. The problem with that strategy was that she didn't want to cause problems for anyone else. She'd read somewhere that suicide was only passing along the grief. Emily knew that if she went missing during the wilderness trip the other campers and Big John would look for her. It would be very traumatic for one of the other kids to find her lifeless body hanging from a branch. They might need therapy. She hated the thought of being responsible for something like that.

The perfect solution would have been to intentionally drown while crossing the lake, but she'd been in too much of a panic to realize it at the time. Nobody wants to burn to death, and while fleeing the fire her survival instincts had completely taken over. Besides, she was responsible for Buttons' safety and it would have been cruel to let him drown or suffocate in the cooler.

What to do next? In the morning she could walk into the forest with her rope and find a sturdy tree. The surrounding bush was thick. It was possible she wouldn't be found for years. Maybe never. Another possibility was to tie something heavy around her waist and walk into the lake. Once again her body might never be found. People would assume she'd died in the forest fire. But that would certainly lead to fingers being pointed at Big John.

She thought again about trying to find pen and paper and leaving a note saying she'd survived the fire but had committed suicide the next day. At least people wouldn't blame Big John.

Another problem was what to do with the small white dog that was pressed against her. When she was gone there would be nobody to look after Buttons. Perhaps she could lock the poodle in the shack with a bowl of water and the last of the food. In the note she could explain why the dog was there and how to track down its owners. The flaw with that plan was there was nothing of value in the cabin and it might take the owners a long time to get around to coming back and checking on things. Buttons might end up starving to death.

What about the big log cabin? The owners were obviously very protective of it. Otherwise they wouldn't have posted so many threatening No Trespassing signs. As soon as it was safe those owners would surely check the property to ensure everything was okay. There would almost certainly be something inside she could use to write a note. She convinced herself there would be a lot of canned and dried food stored inside the cabin. That would allow her to open some cans of tuna or stew, or whatever they had, for Buttons. With food and a pail of water the poodle could probably survive comfortably for a week or more.

Unfortunately the cabin was locked up like a fortress. Getting inside would not be easy. Maybe she could use the axe to break down the door? Emily didn't like the idea of damaging someone else's property, but there didn't appear to be an alternative.

Emily considered her options for a long time, stroking the dog's head the whole while. Yes, breaking into the log cabin seemed to be the best solution. There had to be a lot of supplies stored inside. She could leave food and water for Buttons and let him have the run of the cabin. Surely it wouldn't be long before someone rescued him.

Usually when she came up with a plan she felt better. Not this time. The combination of smoke, several painful burns, and dark thoughts had left her with a fierce headache. Exhausted Emily closed her eyes and cried herself to sleep.

Nine

I t wasn't a restful nap. Her left eye, the one that had been hit by a flying ember, was swollen almost shut and ached dreadfully. Buttons insisted on lying on Emily's chest. Not only did the dog stink of smoke and muck, but having even a small weight on her chest made it harder for Emily to get comfortable.

Then there were the nightmares. Fire demons were chasing her. No matter how fast she ran, or where she turned, she couldn't escape. They were armed with plumes of smoke that turned into nooses. Finally they caught her and attempted to strangle her with the ropes of smoke. In her dreams she kept on fighting and didn't surrender.

One of the fire demons started barking. The barking grew louder and more frantic. It seemed so real that it woke her up. It was no dream. Buttons was in hysterics.

"Leave me alone!" ordered Emily, groggy from pain and exhaustion. But Buttons wouldn't let up. The dog licked Emily's face and his tongue touched the sore eye, causing her to sit up and shriek in pain.

Her first instinct was to swat him, something she would normally never even think of doing. Then, as she became more alert, she realized something was seriously wrong.

The wind was now raging with an intensity she had never imagined possible. The walls of the flimsy shack creaked and groaned. The entire structure appeared to be in danger of flying away. A steady stream of leaves and branches pelted the roof.

Both candles had burned out. Emily fumbled for the flashlight, found it, and used the beam to look around the cabin. The walls shook every time they were hit by a strong gust. There was a deafening crash. Something heavy had landed on the cabin's roof. Emily jumped to her feet and ran for the door. Buttons tried to follow, but Emily feared he would panic again and run into the night. She firmly shoved the dog aside with a foot, slipped outside, and closed the door behind her.

The wind was so strong she had to hold onto a tree to keep upright. Even without using the flashlight she could see that the top of the tree had broken off and landed on the roof, ripping open a hole.

The gale had brought new life to the forest fire. Ferocious winds were fanning the flames and the other side of the lake had become an inferno. It was a wall of fire that seemed to stretch forever. As Emily watched in disbelief the tallest flames joined together and began to whirl around. It was the most awe-inspiring and chilling thing she had ever seen — a tornado made of fire.

The fiery whirlwind seemed to be alive. It went spinning across the land, consuming everything in its path. It halted at the lake's edge and the bottom of the funnel moved erratically back and forth, as if seeking food. For some reason the word *firenado* came into Emily's head. Had she just made it up, or had she actually heard that term before?

Then the *firenado* seemed to make up its mind about where to go next. It moved on to the lake's surface and headed directly toward Emily. It was as if one of the fiery devils from her nightmares had seen her standing on the shore and was determined to devour her. There was no possible escape. It looked as unstoppable as a locomotive. Emily wanted to turn and flee, but terror caused her legs to go numb. She fell to her knees and held up her hands in surrender.

At the precise moment she gave up all hope the towering flames started to lose their intensity. There was no fuel on the lake's surface — the fiery tornado disappeared in just a few seconds.

Discovering that her legs were working once again, Emily got up and turned to run. The flames of the *firenado* may have died but the intensity of the wind hadn't diminished. Just before reaching the cabin she was knocked violently to the ground by a massive cloud of swirling ash.

A flock of sparks landed all around. The lake wasn't wide enough to ensure safety after all. It wouldn't be long before some of those embers started new fires. Emily understood that the surrounding forest would swiftly become a death trap for any living thing caught in it. Once again the lake appeared to offer the only hope of escape. She had to get into the boathouse.

The cooler was lying next to the spot where Emily had fallen. She already knew the container floated well. It was also large enough to hold a lot of supplies. She got to her feet and carried the cooler it into the cabin, where she was greeted by a frantic Buttons. The dog sensed danger all around and wouldn't stop barking.

Using the flashlight to find her way around the shack Emily grabbed everything she could think of that might prove useful. She threw matches, emergency candles, condensed milk, beef jerky, a can opener, and all the spare batteries into the cooler. As she moved the beam of light from her small flashlight around the cabin it suddenly illuminated the ball cap and jacket hanging on the wall. She put on the cap and jacket, hoping they'd offer some protection from flying embers.

Emily placed the cooler next to the door and went back outside. Once again Buttons attempted to follow. Not wanting to run the risk of losing the dog she shoved him back inside and hoped the flimsy door wouldn't blow open.

Then she picked up the axe, aimed the flashlight at the ground, and ran toward the one place that seemed to offer a chance of escape.

Ten

aving made the trip several times, Emily she was able to make good progress, even in the dark. As she got nearer to the big cabin she saw the first flames.

A tree next to the cabin was blazing from top to bottom. The flames leaped to another tree and then to the roof.

Emily knew there was a Jet Ski inside the boathouse. She'd seen it through the window. Hopefully they weren't complicated to operate. If Emily could figure out how to get the machine going and into the water it should be possible to drive back to the shack, grab Buttons, and speed to the middle of the lake. Until she got into the boathouse Emily wouldn't know what was actually inside. The building was large and she'd only been able to see a small part of the interior through the window. It was even possible there was a small fishing boat inside.

Raising the axe above her head, Emily hit the door as hard as she could. The blade wasn't sharp and all it did was take a small gouge out of the wood. She struck a second blow. Once again it only scratched the surface. At this rate it would take an hour to smash through the door. Then she recalled that on television and in the movies people always kicked doors near the handle when they wanted to force their way in.

Using the blunt side of the axe head she hit next to the door handle as hard as she could. There was the sound of breaking metal and splintering wood. She hit it again. The doorframe was definitely coming apart. One more blow and she was inside.

As she used the flashlight to search the boat house her hopes evaporated. There wasn't a boat. Even worse, the Jet Ski she'd pinned her hopes on was useless. The engine was in pieces on the floor.

Emily remembered the canoe back at the shack, but she couldn't recall seeing any paddles. The only thing she knew about canoes was that they were supposed to be very tippy and the prospect of going on the lake in one, especially without a paddle, seemed foolhardy.

She took another look around the building. There were a lot of life jackets hanging from pegs on the wall. She grabbed two adult and one child-size.

The workbench was littered with tools, most of which Emily didn't recognize and had no use for. The only thing of interest was a filleting knife in a sheath. She grabbed it as she headed out the door.

Emily had only been inside the boathouse for a few minutes, but a lot had happened. As she stepped outside her eyes were drawn to the nearby log cabin. Its roof was ablaze and she was certain it wouldn't be long before the entire structure was on fire.

Emily started to run back toward the shack where she'd left Buttons, but stopped in her tracks. She'd just remembered the oar that had helped keep her head above water during the swim across the lake. It was designed for rowing, and was too long to make a good paddle, but was better than nothing. It had come ashore with her near the boathouse ramp. Luckily it was still there. Her arms were full of life jackets, so she tucked the oar under one arm, and headed back to the shack.

Once again Emily found herself in a race with fire. Trees were bursting into flames on both sides of the path. She was grateful for the extra protection from sparks provided by the cap and jacket. It was tough to move quickly because she was dragging the oar and finding it difficult to run in the oversized flip-flops she'd found outside the log cabin.

A shocking sight was waiting for her at the shack. The back wall was on fire. Emily screamed. Buttons was still inside. So was the cooler full of emergency supplies. She dropped her load, pulled open the door, and was relieved to see the poodle race out of the building. She grabbed him before he could run away. Holding Buttons under an arm she reached inside and grabbed the cooler. The interior of the cabin was thick with smoke.

She'd rescued the dog and the supplies. Now Emily had to save the only thing that might offer escape. The canoe was stored between the cabin and a large pile of dried firewood. If it wasn't moved immediately it would be destroyed.

Struggling to control the hysterical dog, Emily remembered the knife she'd taken from the boathouse. She'd shoved it into a coat pocket. With one hand she pulled the slender knife from its sheath and slashed at the clothesline she'd put up earlier in the day. The blade was sharp and easily sliced through the rope. She took one of the loose ends and tied it to the dog's collar. Buttons pulled at the rope, but the knot held.

It looked as though the canoe hadn't been moved in years. Emily ripped off the weathered sheet of canvas that covered it. The canoe was made of aluminum and appeared ancient. She gave it a yank. It wouldn't move. It was chained to a tree. Emily took a quick look at the lock. It was large and solid. She couldn't believe her bad luck. The people who owned the shack hadn't bothered to lock or hide anything else. Why would they lock up a decrepit canoe? It wasn't fair!

The fire had spread to the woodpile and the heat was becoming unbearable. Mind racing, Emily figured she and Buttons would have to go swimming once again. At least they had some life jackets this time. With fires burning on both shores she would probably have to seek shelter in the very middle of the lake. Hopefully the life jackets would keep the two of them afloat. They might have to stay in the water all night.

She put on one of the life jackets as quickly as she could, although her fumbling fingers had difficulty with one of the snaps. Emily looked for Buttons. The dog had backed as far away from the blazing cabin as the rope would allow. She was just about to cut the poodle free when she remembered something. The key! There was a key under the cutlery tray. It had struck her as odd when she'd found it because nothing on the property seemed to be worth stealing. Did the key in the drawer open the padlock that secured the canoe?

The back of the cabin was now fully engulfed and smoke poured out of the open door. Emily had learned about fire safety in elementary school. She knew you were never supposed to go into a burning building. You could die of asphyxiation because of the smoke, or the entire building could collapse on your head.

She hesitated for a moment. There was no guarantee the key in the drawer would even open the padlock. On the other hand, the drawer was tantalizingly close to the front door. All she had to do was duck inside, turn to the left, take two steps, and the drawer was right there. There wasn't time to think things through. Emily had to make an immediate decision.

She steeled herself, took a deep breath, and rushed into the shack. The interior was completely filled with smoke. Almost instantly it blinded her. The extreme heat was painful. It took every ounce of courage she had to keep from turning around and running outside. Blindly, she stumbled toward where she thought the drawer was located. Her fingers touched the countertop. The drawer should be right underneath. It wasn't there. Finally her hands located the metal handle. She pulled it open and then yanked out the cutlery tray. The crash of spoons and forks hitting the wooden floor was nearly drowned out by the crackle of flames.

The key was somewhere at the bottom of the drawer, but Emily couldn't see anything. Smoke and her own tears blinded her. She'd never been good at holding her breath and was rapidly reaching her limit, but knew that breathing in smoke would be fatal. Suddenly she felt very unsteady on her feet. Time had run out. She was about to faint. Her fingers finally located the key. She grabbed it, turned, and tripped over the cutlery tray.

She hit the ground hard, convinced the end had come. To her astonishment she discovered there was a narrow layer of breathable air close to the floor. Gasping, holding on to the precious key for dear life, she felt a draft. That must be where the door was. She'd barely made it outside when part of the roof caved in.

Still half-blinded by the smoke Emily staggered to the canoe and discovered the aluminum skin was already warm. In a few moments it might be too hot to touch. The canoe was chained to a tree and the top of that tree was now burning furiously. She grabbed the lock, inserted the key, and twisted. The lock was rusty and didn't want to open, but Emily yanked on it with strength she didn't know she had. It opened with a metallic screech.

She dropped the chain on the ground, grabbed the bow of the canoe, and pulled. It would have been too heavy for her to carry on her own, but the narrow boat slid easily over the ground. After pulling it some distance from the blazing shack Emily starting throwing things into it. The two extra life jackets, the cooler full of emergency supplies, the axe and the oar were tossed haphazardly inside. Then she cut the rope restraining Buttons. Holding the struggling poodle under one arm, and pulling the canoe with her other hand, she staggered to the lake. The fire hadn't yet reached the trees nearest to the beach. Otherwise Emily wouldn't have had any hope of escape.

After reaching the beach Emily shoved the front of the canoe into the water. There were two seats, one in the front and one in the back. They had wooden frames and canvas webbing. In the middle of the canoe was a narrow board that ran crosswise, just like the seats did.

There was still a length of rope attached to Buttons' collar. Emily used it to tie the dog to the front seat. She didn't want him to run off at the last minute. Luckily the poodle cowered at the bottom of the boat.

Using the oar for balance Emily stepped into the canoe and sat down awkwardly. The canoe was still in the shallows, but already rocked from side to side. Desperate to leave the beach Emily used the oar as a pole until it was no longer long enough to reach the lake bottom. Then she started using it as a paddle. It was awkward to use, because of its length, but it worked.

Emily heard a tremendous crash, looked back, and saw the walls of the shack collapse. If Buttons hadn't woken her she might still be inside.

Eleven

It took less than a minute for Emily to realize the canoe might not be her salvation. It was even tippier than she'd expected. The light craft was almost unmanageable in the strong wind. With each gust it skittered across the surface like a panicked horse. Emily discovered that even if she paddled as hard as she could it was barely enough to keep her more than a few metres from the shore. All the trees along the shoreline were aflame. If the canoe were blown to land it would be a catastrophe. Overcome with frustration she began screaming every insult she could think of at the fire. The temper tantrum ended when Emily was startled into silence by a number of loud bangs.

The noise seemed to come from the big log cabin, now clearly visible from the canoe. The cabin was completely engulfed in flames. It sounded like fireworks going off inside the building. Then Emily remembered all of the threatening No Trespassing signs posted on the property, including the one featuring a picture of a gun. If they'd stored ammunition somewhere inside, it would explain the sound of explosions.

Afraid of being hit by a stray bullet she put her head down and put every ounce of energy she still had into paddling.

The sky, lake, and land were suddenly bathed in blue light. The air crackled with electricity. There was a painfully loud bang that sounded like the cracking of a giant whip. A lightning bolt had hit nearby. The thunderstorm the radio station had warned about was now a reality. Emily didn't know much about wilderness survival, but she realized that being in a metal boat on a lake was probably one of the worst places you could possibly be during a lightning storm.

There were two more lightning strikes in rapid succession, although they weren't as close. The wind continued to blow the canoe further down the lake. Emily paddled clumsily in an attempt to stay a safe distance from the flames. She passed another burning cabin. It stood on a heavily wooded point that jutted into the lake and was directly in her path. The canoe was headed toward the most intense part of the inferno.

Emily now had a tiny amount of practical experience in how to steer the canoe, although every time she aimed the bow toward the middle of the lake the light craft was tossed around by the gale. It was impossible to go in a straight line. She leaned forward and paddled until her arms felt like they were going to fall off. A single blazing tree, surrounded by large rocks, stood at the very tip of the point.

A sudden gust did her a great favour by momentarily driving the canoe away from the shore. Emily could barely see through her swollen and sweat-drenched eyes, but sensed she might be on the verge of safely passing into open water.

The flaming tree was still much too close for comfort. When the canoe was halfway past it another blast of wind caught the craft and pushed it back toward the flames. She looked up and saw burning branches less than a metre above her head. In a panic she used the oar to try and push the canoe back into deeper water. Unfortunately the lake bottom was muck and it swallowed the wooden blade. Trying to pull out the oar actually pulled the boat closer to the burning tree. The fire was so hot it felt as though her skin was beginning to crackle.

In desperation she pushed the blade of the oar into the trunk of the tree. There was a sickening crash. The tree was rotten and it cracked at the very spot where the oar rammed into it. The top half of the tree swayed in the fierce wind. The scene seemed to play out in slow motion. The burning tree was falling directly toward her. Once again Emily lunged desperately with the oar. The blade hit something solid. The front of the canoe turned away from the shore. The trunk narrowly missed her head before hitting the side of the canoe.

Twelve

Emily felt as though she were being cooked alive. The heat was unbearable, so when the canoe overturned and she went into the water it came as a relief. The life jacket prevented her head from going under the water and she bobbed around, dazed, trying to make sense of what had just happened. The broken tree trunk that had overturned the canoe floated nearby. She heard the hiss of the last flames being extinguished by the lake water.

The canoe floated well upside down. It rode high enough in the water to provide some protection from the nearby fire. Buttons was barking furiously. Emily could hear her companion's nails scratching across aluminum, but at first she couldn't figure out where the dog had gone. Then it dawned on her that Buttons was trapped underneath the canoe and was still tied to the seat.

Emily gook a deep breath and tried to duck under the canoe and reach the dog. The life jacket was so buoyant that she couldn't get her head under the surface. As she thrashed the water in frustration her feet touched bottom. She'd stumbled upon a sand bar. Her toes eagerly pressed into the packed sand and it dawned on her that both flip-flops had fallen off when she went into the water. Her ball cap had also come off.

The water was up to her neck, but being able to stand allowed Emily to lift the side of the canoe and crawl under it. Buttons had managed to climb partway onto one of the seats and she decided he was not in imminent danger of drowning. Emily discovered that the overturned boat not only shielded her from the fury of the fire that raged just a few metres away, but that it contained a large air pocket. She could breathe comfortably. That was the good news. Unfortunately all her emergency gear had been lost, except for the small life jacket that had somehow got tangled up in a seat.

With nothing between her and the nearest flames except a thin aluminum wall, Emily pointed the bow of the canoe toward deeper water. She walked as far as she could and when the bottom fell away she held onto the centre cross piece and started kicking. The overturned vessel didn't move smoothly through the water, but that turned out to be an advantage. The wind didn't move it around as easily as when the canoe was floating on its bottom.

There were lots of shallow areas along that strip of lakeshore. Emily's feet often touched muck or rock and she was able to push the canoe along at a steady place. Although Buttons wouldn't stop whining he had managed to wedge himself into a secure perch. Only his hindquarters dragged in the water.

Emily would periodically stop and lift the canoe letting air inside and allowing her to keep an eye on what was happening outside the metal cocoon. The lightning and thunder continued, although there wasn't yet any rain. The radio had warned that lightning strikes could make the fire situation a lot worse unless they were accompanied by heavy rain.

Most of the shoreline was a continuous wall of flames, but there was a small strip of darkness immediately ahead. It was a mystery. But then it occurred to her that if there was land in front of her that wasn't on fire it must mean that it was made out of something that couldn't burn. Although it was too dark to see what she was getting into she decided to take the gamble. She turned toward the blackness and wearily began kicking. Emily felt her body had already been through too much that day. It was all she could do to hold onto the canoe.

Something hard banged against the side of the canoe and Emily's heart fluttered. She wondered what fresh disaster she'd have to face. Whatever was waiting outside bumped against the boat for a second time.

With difficulty she managed to duck her head under the water, come up outside the canoe, and come face-to-face with the cooler. And it was floating just an arm's length away. The wind and waves had taken it away. Now they were giving it back. It felt like Christmas morning. All her survival gear was inside the container. It was floating low in the water because there were some heavy things inside, but she was amazed it was still floating at all. The cooler was now the most valuable thing in the world to her, and she wasn't going to risk losing it again.

Then came another piece of luck. Her feet hit ground, allowing her to stand up and pull the cooler under the canoe.

Several minutes later, after alternating between walking and swimming, her toes pressed into slime. Once again she stopped to peek out at the world and renew the air supply. She had arrived in a shadowy place that had been mysteriously spared, even though it was surrounded on three sides by fire. There was a sharp, rotten smell that even partially masked the stink of smoke. Night had fallen and, with the smoke blocking any light from the moon and stars, Emily couldn't see anything except some sinister shadows. At least the shadows weren't moving.

The water was quite shallow, although the mud was deep and seemed determined to drag her down. Every footstep required energy she no longer had. Emily came out from under the canoe and started pulling it awkwardly through the muck. Buttons was still underneath and wasn't happy about it.

"Stop whining," ordered Emily. "I don't know if we're safe or if we're already dead and gone to hell."

Thirteen

Emily grabbed fistfuls of vegetation that felt like wet sponge, and pulled. She was in waist-deep muck, trying desperately to haul herself onto something that appeared to be land. It was as if the muddy lake bottom didn't want to let her go. After an exhausting struggle Emily was able to free her legs and crawl up the bank.

As she stood up the ground quivered. It felt like soggy carpet to her bare feet. Emily had heard of muskeg and she wondered if that's what she was walking on. If so it meant she'd landed in the middle of a swamp, and that would explain why there weren't any flames nearby.

Walking was difficult because the ground was so unstable. Fighting to keep her balance, Emily tried to pull the canoe onto shore. The boat was still upside down, with Buttons trapped inside the hull, making her job harder. After she got the canoe onto its side she was able to drag it and a very unhappy poodle out of the lake.

Emily knelt on the moss, alert for danger. She started to take off the life jacket, but changed her mind. It seemed possible they'd still have to flee at a moment's notice.

She picked up the cooler, took off the lid, and reached inside. The contents were all jumbled, but at least they were dry. After fumbling around she found the flashlight. The narrow beam of light wasn't able to penetrate very far into the smoke and inky darkness, but it did provide enough illumination to reveal they were on an island that was no bigger than her backyard at home. There was hardly any vegetation, except for the moss, some spindly saplings, and a few cattails. Emily had never been in a swamp before and decided it would normally be the last place on earth she'd want to be. She pulled up a handful of moss and was pleasantly surprised by how much water oozed out of it. It seemed impossible that something that wet could ever catch on fire.

Because they were on an island, and there really wasn't anywhere to go, Emily figured it was safe to untie Buttons. He showed no interest in wandering off. Instead the poodle huddled next to the canoe, seeking shelter from the wind. Occasionally he'd sniff the air and whine.

Emily realized she was thirsty. Although it seemed she'd been in the lake all day she'd hardly had anything to drink. The two cans of evaporated milk were still in the cooler, but they were small and she was reluctant to open them so soon. She crawled to the shore, intending to get a drink. The water smelled vile. She reluctantly scooped up some in her hands and drank it. It tasted even worse than it smelled. She forced herself to take another couple of gulps before deciding the swamp water was going to make her sick if she drank any more.

She'd just made it back to the canoe when Buttons went nuts. It was hard to believe that such ferocious barks and growls could come out of a pampered house pet. Emily couldn't see anything, but thought she might have heard a faint splash. If there was something moving in the swamp the poodle's barking was drowning out the noise. Emily was just about to tell the poodle to shut up when she heard something sloshing through the water. Instantly alarmed she turned on the flashlight. She pointed the beam of light in the same direction the poodle was looking. At first she couldn't see anything. Then a large, dark body came out of the water and two eyes gleamed in the light. The eyes were staring right at her. The creature was silent for a few moments before making an odd moaning sound. The eyes were suddenly gone. Moments later they reappeared, only they were higher off the ground. Emily gasped, unable to make sense of it. Then it dawned on her that whatever was watching her had stood up to get a better look.

The flashlight finally lit up the animal enough for Emily to see what she was dealing with and it was nearly enough to cause her to faint from fear. A bear stood on its hind legs, swaying from side to side and sniffing the air. It growled when Emily aimed her light directly at its eyes. Terrified, she turned off the flashlight.

Emily knew there were both black and grizzly bears in British Columbia. She wouldn't have been able to tell which kind she was dealing with, even if she could have seen it clearly. All she knew was that she was terrified of bears. It didn't matter if it was a black bear or a grizzly. She'd read enough news stories to know that both types were known to attack and kill people. Sometimes they even ate their victims.

Emily's initial instinct was to push the canoe back into the water and escape the island. Then she remembered losing the oar when the canoe overturned. It was still floating somewhere in the dark. There was nothing to use as a paddle or pole. There was no escape. If the bear charged it would be on her in seconds.

The animal snorted again. It appeared to be coming closer, although without turning on the flashlight it was impossible to tell for certain. Emily reached into the cooler and grabbed the knife. Despite her terror she was determined to fight. With the flashlight in one hand and the knife in the other Emily instinctively moved behind the canoe so that it was between her and the bear. Then she had a flash of inspiration. If an overturned canoe could provide shelter in the water it might do the same thing on land.

Convinced the bear was about to attack, Emily dropped the knife and clenched the small flashlight in her teeth. Having freed her hands she flipped the canoe over. Buttons was so startled by her actions that he stopped barking. Emily lifted up the stern, pushed the dog to safety, and then slid under herself. The canoe was long enough that she was able to stretch out on the damp ground.

The flashlight revealed there were spaces between the overturned boat and the earth that were big enough for a bear to shove a paw into. Then she discovered the soggy ground could also work in her favour. Her weight, pressing down on the thin wooden board that ran across the middle of the canoe, was enough to push the sides into the moss, eliminating most of the cracks. She turned off the flashlight, fearing it would help the bear find whatever gaps remained.

The bear approached slowly, moaning and clicking its teeth. Its feet made a squishing sound as the large animal sank into the moss with every step. Buttons pressed himself against the front of the canoe and whimpered.

The footsteps abruptly stopped. Emily wondered if the bear had stopped moving or if it was just on drier ground. She knew she'd dropped the knife, but wasn't sure if it had ended up under the boat with her. It was the only weapon she had and she desperately wanted to find it. As quietly as possible, Emily searched her tiny sanctuary for the knife. It was pitch black, and there was hardly any room to move, so she blindly ran her hands over the ground and along the sides of the canoe. Nothing.

After a few minutes she reluctantly turned on the flashlight, hoping the light wouldn't attract the bear. There was no sign of the knife.

Close to her head was a narrow opening where the canoe and muskeg didn't quite form a seal. Emily pressed her cheek hard against the ground and aimed the flashlight's beam outside. An arm's length away, gleaming in the light, was the missing blade. Right next to it was the face of a bear. It growled and blinked in the light. Emily dropped the flashlight and pressed down on the canoe as hard as she could, hoping to press it further into the moss and eliminate all remaining cracks.

The bear circled the canoe several times, sniffing and moaning. It gave the boat a shove. Emily felt the walls move and heard the scratch of claws. She nearly fainted from fright. Then, for no apparent reason, the bear moved off. She could clearly hear its footsteps sloshing through the muck and moss.

Wondering if she was taking a reckless gamble, Emily waited for a minute and then slid out from under the canoe. On her knees, she used the flashlight to look for the bear. She heard an annoyed woof and saw the gleaming eyes. The beast was on the far side of the small island.

Knowing that if the animal attacked she didn't have a second to spare Emily grabbed the cooler, knife and small life jacket. She dragged them to safety under the canoe.

Although she was glad to rescue her gear it meant there was even less room to move around in the aluminum cocoon. She awkwardly pushed the small life jacket to the bow and made a bed for the dog.

"I was going to try and turn this into a life jacket for you," she said. The poodle didn't make a peep.

Emily pointed the light at Buttons, concerned about his condition. The dog was wet, filthy and so tired he could barely sit up. Remarkably, the pink ribbon was still in place.

Satisfied that the dog wasn't injured Emily stretched out on the musty moss. She was utterly spent and her left eye was swollen shut. The eyelid and the surrounding skin were too sore to touch. Emily didn't think the eye itself had been damaged, but couldn't be sure. When she laid the side of her face onto the cool ground it brought some relief. After a while she simply pulled up a fistful of moss and held it gently against the injured eye. It helped a little.

Without the bear snuffling around the shelter Emily was able to relax a little. In addition to the sore eye there were several other burns, a gash on the back of her right hand that she couldn't explain, and her arms and legs throbbed. It felt like every muscle in her body had been strained or torn.

Fourteen

When it finally started to rain it was as if a giant tap had been turned on. A torrent of raindrops hit the aluminum hull with such force that the sound was like being inside a giant drum. Emily checked her watch. It was after midnight. Even before the rain the wildfire had appeared to be slowly dying down. A lot of the available fuel, especially the dead trees and dried pine needles on the forest floor, had already been consumed. There were still flames everywhere, but Emily suspected the situation might be better in the morning. Hopefully the bear would be gone by then. She had no idea what would happen if it was still hanging around. She couldn't stay under the canoe forever.

Almost as suddenly as the rain started, it stopped. The deluge hadn't been long enough or intense enough to put out the fire. Emily hoped the rain would come again, but she waited in vain. She'd been wondering if there were some way to safely capture some of the rainwater.

The swamp water hadn't satisfied her thirst. Her throat was so dry she could barely swallow. Emily craved something clean to drink. The only liquid available was condensed milk. There were two cans in the cooler, which was lying on the ground next to the top of her head.

The cooler was so large it barely fit under the canoe. Getting it open wasn't easy. She had to turn onto her stomach and unlock the lid, forcing her to momentarily lift up the back of the canoe. Fortunately the bear wasn't sniffing around.

Emily slid the top off the cooler and reached blindly inside. Her hand went from one object to the next, trying to identify every last piece of her meagre survival supplies. She found a can of condensed milk and the can opener. The tin felt disappointingly light in her hand. There wasn't much liquid in it. Emily decided to limit herself to one can of milk. She'd save the second tin for later.

After carefully opening the can she pressed it to her lips and started sipping. She wanted to make it last as long as possible, but her body craved the sweet liquid and the sips turned into gulps. In what seemed like the blink of an eye the can was empty. She set it down and Buttons' nose was suddenly inside.

The dog frantically licked up any drops of liquid that were still inside the can. He whimpered for more. Buttons was as desperate for food and drink as Emily was. At first the dog's begging annoyed her. Then she felt ashamed for drinking the entire can of milk herself. Emily reminded herself that she and the poodle were a team. They had to look out for each other. That meant they had to share whatever supplies they had.

Emily found the second can of milk and opened it. Buttons sensed it was for him and barked eagerly. Emily couldn't resist taking another gulp, but she gave the rest to the poodle. It was a fair amount of liquid for a small dog, but Buttons didn't stop until it was gone.

It came as a surprise to Emily to discover she was getting chilled. The day had been scorching hot and the night wasn't much cooler, but she'd spent hours in the water and her clothes were still soaking wet. And now she was lying on top of damp moss. It felt as if the heat were being drained from her body.

Emily was still wearing the life jacket, which kept her torso from touching the ground and also provided some insulation. Buttons hadn't shown any interest in bedding down on the child-size life jacket. Emily took it for herself. She spread it out and used it as protection for her hips. The cooler lid wasn't serving a useful purpose for anything, so she slid it under her feet. Most of her body was now off the muskeg, although the bed could hardly be called comfortable.

Annoyingly, her elbow kept hitting the two empty milk cans. Her first instinct was to toss them outside, but it occurred to her that the smell of food might attract the bear. Then she remembered that empty cans could be useful in an emergency.

Her mother had been raised in northern BC, where winter roads are often treacherous. A mechanical breakdown in the middle of nowhere might be fatal. Motorists can freeze if they don't have a source of heat. Emily's mother always kept a simple survival kit in the trunk of her car in the winter. The kit included an empty can, emergency candles that are designed to burn all night, and matches. Emily had been told that if you lit the candle, put it into a tin can, and held the can on your lap it provided both light and warmth.

Emily was skeptical that it would actually work, but she had all the necessary material and nothing to lose. The milk tins were smaller than the coffee can her mother kept in the winter survival kit. Emily wasn't sure if that was a good or bad thing.

She put her hand back into the cooler and fumbled around until she found everything she needed. Emily used a match to light a candle and poured a little hot wax into the can. She stuck the bottom of the candle into the wax and was pleased to see it remained upright. The candle did provide some welcome light and she could feel the can gradually getting warmer in her hands.

Emily thought about lighting a second one, but concluded it wouldn't provide enough extra heat or light to make it worthwhile. After a while the poodle climbed on top of her, so she set the can on the ground, next to her head, and watched the flame. Was it her imagination or was it gradually getting a little warmer in the shelter? She had another empty can and a lot of candles, so there was nothing to lose. Emily lit a second candle and placed it next to the first one.

Gently pressing moss against her swollen eye, and breathing deeply, Emily tried to get some rest. She was starting to feel a little better when she heard a familiar high-pitched whine that never failed to make her skin crawl. Unbelievably, there was a mosquito trapped with her under the canoe. Every other flying insect in the forest had probably been killed or driven away by the flames and smoke, but one hardy survivor had managed to find her. The little bloodsucker undoubtedly lived in the swamp and Emily's overturned canoe was providing it with exactly the shelter it needed. Shelter *and* a meal. Emily knew she was going to get bitten. It was inevitable. The bite would swell and itch horribly. As if she didn't have enough to worry about already.

The buzz grew louder. Buttons snapped his jaws. The noise stopped instantly. Emily reached out and gave the dog's head a grateful pat. Then she closed her eyes and fell into a restless sleep.

Fifteen

Emily and Buttons awoke at the same moment, although both were too groggy to understand why. Something was wrong. Emily blinked in the gloom. One eye was swollen shut and the other came into focus slower than usual. One of the candles had gone out and the other was only a stub. The remaining flame hardly provided any illumination.

There was an ominous grunt close to her ear. Emily turned her head and her nose nearly touched the bear's snout. The canoe was no longer flush to the ground. Perhaps she had shifted her weight while sleeping, and the bear had found a big enough space to wedge its muzzle inside. It's rancid breath was so close to Emily's face that it caused her to gag. When the bear snorted it sprayed hot snot across her face.

It was Buttons who recovered his senses first. Emily barely had time to scream before the furious poodle threw himself on the oversized nose and bit the sensitive tip. Taken completely by surprise the bear pulled its muzzle out from under the canoe and roared in fury. The thin aluminum hull shivered under several violent blows. Emily was terrified that the animal might figure out how easily it could flip the boat over with its paws. She began yelling at the top of her lungs and banging on the canoe's sides in a desperate attempt to scare the bear off. Buttons added to the racket by barking wildly. The outburst lasted for just a few seconds before they both fell into an exhausted silence. The bear was no longer attacking the canoe. Emily couldn't hear the animal. She knew it might be still lurking nearby, but figured the only way to find out for certain was to lift up the canoe and have a look. She wasn't prepared to take the risk.

Emily picked up the little poodle and hugged it tightly. Once again Buttons had saved her from a horrible fate. The prospect of being eaten by a bear was even worse than being burned alive. It took a long time before she regained enough composure to light another two candles.

She didn't get any more sleep that night. Teeth chattering from the cold and damp, she listened to the distant sound of thunder and constantly checked the time.

The previous morning she'd had to get up at sunrise to leave on the wilderness expedition, so she knew the sun would be up by about 5:00 AM. She wondered if she'd be able to make it that long.

Horrible stomach cramps were making it abundantly clear that drinking the swamp water had been a mistake. The only thing keeping her from doubling over in pain was the fact there wasn't enough room for her to curl up under the canoe.

Buttons whimpered, sensing that something was wrong.

"I have to get outside before it gets really nasty in here," moaned Emily.

Desperate, she lifted the side of the boat, saw no sign of the bear, and rolled outside. The morning sun was weak, but visibility was a little better than it had been the previous day. When she stood up she could see the bear was lying on the other side of the island, barely twenty metres away. It didn't even raise its head to look at her. Emily wondered if the animal was dead. She hoped it was, because she was suffering from a horrendous bout of diarrhea. Her stomach was churning because of a mixture of swamp water and fear of a bear attack. She ducked behind a nearby clump of cattails and tried to keep an eye on the unwelcome visitor.

It wasn't until she was finally able to stand up again that Emily had the presence of mind to take note of her surroundings.

The worst of the fire was over. Endless ranks of charcoal skeletons had replaced the green forest. Many trees were still burning, although the horizon was no longer a solid mass of flames. It was difficult to see exactly what was happening on the other side of the lake, although there seemed to be even fewer flames over there. The smoke was still thick enough to prevent a pilot flying overhead to spot her. Then it occurred to her that she was increasingly focused on making it out alive.

The bear stirred.

"We have to get out of here," said Emily. She flipped the canoe onto its bottom and threw Buttons and all her possessions inside. Then she pushed it to the water's edge. She looked around desperately for something to use as a paddle. There was nothing. Then she noticed a dead sapling lying on the ground. She picked it up. The wood felt spongy. Emily would have to depend on a rotten pole barely taller than she was. Her movements had attracted the attention of the bear, now sitting up awkwardly and watching her.

Terrified the bear was about to attack, Emily jumped into the canoe and clumsily pushed off. The pole was too short to be of much use and the jagged base drove deep into the muck at the swamp's bottom. She was hardly able to make any headway at first. Every few seconds she turned her head to see what the bear was doing. It could barely get to its feet. It looked like the animal had a badly burned rear paw that would have steadily become more painful overnight. It might also explain why it hadn't tried harder to flip over the canoe to get at her. The bear silently watched her leave.

Now that she'd had a better look she decided it was probably a black bear and not a grizzly. It certainly wasn't as large as she'd imagined it to be. Perhaps it had never meant her any harm. Still, she couldn't breathe normally or stop trembling until she was some distance from the bear and the island.

Sixteen

It took nearly ten minutes to pole out of the swamp, something that would have taken less than a minute with a proper paddle. As soon as they reached open water Emily dipped one of the milk tins into the lake and drank deeply. The water tasted like a mixture of smoke and candle wax, but it quenched her thirst.

"I think we'd be better off on the other side of the lake," said Emily. "We know there are roads over there. That's also where people are most likely to look for us." Buttons barked in agreement. He was also glad to leave the stinking marsh and the bear.

Emily didn't like the idea of trying to cross the lake without a paddle. She gingerly pushed the boat along the lakeshore, knowing the fragile pole wouldn't take much stress, and hoping she'd spot the missing oar. It was now quite safe to hug the shoreline. There were plenty of burning logs and smoldering stumps, but there was no longer any imminent danger of being roasted.

Her biggest concern was the condition of the canoe. It was leaking badly. If the battered old boat had been taking on water the previous evening she hadn't noticed in all the turmoil. She figured that being swatted by an enraged bear probably hadn't done the bottom any good, especially if it was already leaky. Emily realized she needed a bailing can. The two milk tins were still in the boat, but they were too small to be of any use.

She decided that going to shore and abandoning the canoe would force her to walk through a hot wasteland where danger lurked at every step. Emily did not look forward to the prospect. It seemed better to occasionally take the boat into shallow water and empty it by turning it over.

Eventually she came to the ruins of the little shack that had provided her with temporary shelter and a handful of supplies. All that remained was the stove and the metal frames of the old couch and mattresses. The people who owned it obviously didn't have much money. She wondered if they would be able to rebuild, or even if they would want to.

She continued to pole the canoe along the lakeshore, looking in vain for the oar. Emily had just about given up on finding it when she saw something truly amazing. The boathouse had survived the fire. Everything around it was gone. The log cabin was a smoking pile of rubble. For some inexplicable reason the boathouse had made it through the inferno with nothing more than a few scorch marks. It might have been saved by the fact it was beside the lake and there were no nearby trees.

When Emily originally broke into the building she'd been in a panic and didn't have time to take a careful look around. She realized there might be something useful inside that she'd missed in the dark. There might be a paddle, food, another pair of flip-flops, or maybe even some dry clothing.

She landed the canoe at the exact same spot where she'd crawled ashore after swimming across the lake. Emily untied Buttons, trusting him not to wander off on his own. Then she pulled the canoe onto the ramp and turned it onto its side to drain the water.

The Band-Aid on her injured foot was long gone, and all her joints were painfully stiff, so Emily limped badly as she walked on the paving stones that led to the broken door. There still wasn't much light inside, so she turned on her flashlight. It revealed that the overhead door was much like the one at her grandfather's garage. In hardly any time she'd unlocked and opened the big door. As it swung open the light poured in.

Unfortunately there wasn't a paddle or an oar. There were still half a dozen life jackets hanging on a wall and Emily decided they could be useful. She threw them onto the ramp, next to the canoe. There were lots of tools lying on the workbench, but she didn't think wrenches and hammers would be of any use. A single waterski leaned against a wall. She moved it to see if there was anything useful behind it. There wasn't, so she put the ski back.

In one corner was a blue bin filled with recycling. She opened it and found a large tin that had once contained stewed tomatoes. It would make an excellent bailing bucket. She tossed it into the canoe and then put the two condensed milk tins into the recycling bin. It was disappointing not to find more useful stuff inside the boathouse. Emily was just about to give up when she spied a small plastic package on top of the seat of the Jet Ski. Inside was a blue tarp. The package had never been opened. She took it, just in case.

Emily went outside and sat on the ramp. "That was a huge disappointment," she informed the dog. "I was hoping to find something to put on my feet." She sighed. "And you'd think that someone who had the money for a vacation property like this would keep a spare paddle or two in their boathouse."

Buttons got on his hind legs and begged.

"I'll bet you're starved. I'm hungry too, but we don't have much."

There was some beef jerky in the cooler. Emily ate one piece and gave another to the dog. Buttons ate his with gusto and asked for more. "We can each have one more piece. That will leave us with two pieces each. That has to last until we get you back to your parents."

Emily decided that the best thing about beef jerky was that it was so chewy you felt as though you were eating more than you really were. She stretched out on the ramp, staring at the murky sky, and wondered if all the smoke was from BC fires or if some were still coming in from California.

The day was shaping up to be another scorcher and her body was warming up nicely. She took off the life jacket and the old jacket she'd found at the shack and noticed with interest that there were some large burn holes in both. She'd been showered with hot embers on several occasions. The extra layers had saved her from getting a few more nasty burns.

Emily was glad she didn't have a mirror. In addition to her burns and bruises she knew she was filthy. She'd already pulled numerous twigs and bits of moss out of her hair and was positive there was lots she'd missed. All her clothes were caked with muck and stank of swamp and smoke. She decided to give herself and the clothes a quick rinse in the lake. Everything would dry quickly in the oppressive heat, and while she was waiting she could think about what to do next.

She stripped naked and walked gingerly into the lake. There was a pebble bottom that provided secure footing and was pleasant to walk on. Emily took a breath and submerged herself completely. Although the water stung her swollen eye she stayed under as long as she could in hopes of washing away any dirt or moss that might infect it. Then she took her clothes into the lake and rinsed them out as best as she could. After spreading them out to dry she once again stretched out on the boat ramp and felt warmth course through her limbs.

Buttons lay down beside her.

"For someone who wants to end it all I've put an awful lot of effort into staying alive," said Emily. "Sometimes I catch myself daydreaming about being rescued." She chuckled, causing Buttons to wag his tail. "It's all your fault. I've been trying to keep you safe and sound and you've returned the favour. If it wasn't for you I might have burned up inside the shack or been eaten by a bear." She suddenly became thoughtful. "Those are both awful ways to go. And thanks for getting that mosquito. You must have better reflexes than I thought."

Buttons barked proudly and begged for more food.

"Sorry, you'll have to wait a while. We're on strict rations right now."

The smoke still hung heavy over land and water. She was pretty sure that nobody was going to spot them from the air. There would certainly be search parties out looking for them as soon as it was safe to go into the woods. They'd probably focus on the other side of the lake, where Emily had last been seen.

"We could wait right here," she said. Buttons appeared to listen carefully. "We've got a roof over our heads and we could sleep on top of the life jackets. The problem is that it could be days before they check this side of the lake. We don't have any food. Besides, I'm not the most patient person in the world. I'm not good at sitting and waiting. I'd rather do something."

She studied the small dog carefully. It had led a pampered existence and was obviously used to regular meals. She knew people could go a long time without food, but wasn't sure about miniature poodles. Could they starve to death in just a few days? It didn't seem likely, although Emily didn't know. Buttons certainly didn't seem to have much energy. His coat was filthy and he watched her with dull eyes.

"If I can find something to use as a paddle we're going to get to the other side of the lake."

Emily waded along the lakeshore for a while, just in case the oar had finally floated ashore. No luck. Maybe something had survived in the log cabin. The path of paving stones allowed her to walk safely up to the smoldering ruins. Everything had been destroyed. The twisted remnants of a fridge and stove clearly showed where the kitchen had been. The floor was littered with ruined dishes and pots and pans. Stacks of canned goods had fallen over, their labels burned off.

"I bet everything I needed was in there," sighed Emily.

The smell seemed to bother Buttons. He stayed well back. "I should have broken in. Nobody would ever know and I'm sure we'd have lots of food. The place had solar panels so I wouldn't be surprised if there was a phone or two-way radio inside. We could be out of here by now."

Not breaking down the front door had been a huge mistake. Emily had been intimidated by all the No Trespassing signs. As she looked around she noticed that the fire had destroyed all the signs. For some reason that made her feel a little better.

She walked back to the boathouse, determined to take one last look inside. She checked every corner and peered inside the toolbox. Nothing. As she leaned the waterski back against the wall it occurred to her that it might make a decent paddle. She got into the canoe and tried it out. It wasn't as easy to hold onto as a proper paddle, but it definitely worked.

The plastic bindings were a nuisance, so Emily decided to get rid of them. There were lots of screwdrivers on the workbench and she quickly found one that was the right size. She managed to get the bindings off with very little difficulty.

Emily had seen life jackets for pets. Finding the child-size life jacket had given her an idea. She cut off a short piece of her rope and started unraveling it. Soon she was left with several pieces that were no thicker than twine. She used the filleting knife to cut the flotation panels into smaller pieces. Then she used the point of the knife to poke holes in the miniature panels, which were then tied together with twine.

Buttons must have been used to being dressed up because he didn't make the slightest fuss as Emily experimented with fitting the life jacket. The final design consisted of four tiny flotation panels that wrapped around the dog's torso.

"Hopefully we're not going into the drink again," said Emily, "but if we do that should keep you afloat."

Then she used another piece of rope to tie all the spare life jackets together. In an emergency they would make a useful raft. As she was working on one of the life jackets she felt a bulge. She took a closer look and discovered there was a pocket. Emily unzipped the pocket, looked inside, and was delighted to find an unopened energy bar.

She immediately opened it and began eating. Buttons watched enviously and whined. "Okay. I agree it isn't fair that I'm the only one eating. I'm going to give you one more piece of beef jerky."

The poodle happily chewed the meat, although it wasn't enough to truly satisfy him. The energy bar had probably been in the pocket for some time. It tasted stale, but at least it helped fill the void in Emily's stomach.

The clothes she'd spread out were finally dry. Emily was tired of wearing wet clothes and she knew there was a strong probability that at least part of her was going to get soaked again. Crossing a lake in a leaky canoe wasn't the best way to stay dry.

"I think I'm just going to wear my underwear," she said. Although Emily was modest by nature she recognized there wasn't much difference between her underwear and the bathing suits many girls wore. If anything, her undies probably covered up more than their bikinis did.

She folded up her pants, sweatshirt, and the jacket she'd found at the shack and put them inside the cooler. Experience had proven the cooler would keep her emergency supplies dry and it wouldn't sink if it ended up in the lake again. It would do the same for her clothes.

Just one day earlier the thought of trying to get to the other side of the lake in a leaky canoe, and without a proper paddle, would have been terrifying. Now, having crossed that same lake with nothing more than a cooler and chunks of wood to keep afloat, she felt an unfamiliar sense of confidence. There was no doubt in her mind she'd be able to pull it off.

The canoe leaked badly, but at least she now had a big bailing can. The waterski would make a decent paddle. Emily also had a life jacket to wear and several more tied together. She thought a life jacket raft should be more than enough to keep her afloat in an emergency. The wind didn't look as though it was going to be a factor. There was only a gentle breeze, not enough to blow the canoe off course.

Emily stood up and squinted through her one good eye at the blood-red sun. The smoke hadn't thinned as much as she'd hoped. She picked up the poodle and put him in the canoe. Then she pushed off from shore and tightly gripped the ski.

On the opposite side of the lake, shrouded in smoke, was the boat access where she'd first entered the water to flee the wildfire. There was a primitive road leading from the boat launch. If she could find that road it should be possible to hike out. Emily knew she wouldn't get very far walking across a forest of hot coals in bare feet, but a dirt road would probably have cooled off by now. At the very least she'd be on the side of the lake where search crews were likely to look first.

"Here goes nothing," said Emily.

She noticed that Buttons didn't seem happy. His previous trips in the canoe had not ended well. He looked around anxiously and sighed.

Seventeen

The ski did not make a good paddle after all. It was too wide to hold on to comfortably. It was also too short. Emily had to lean uncomfortably far over the side to thrust the ski into the water. It wasn't long before her arm muscles, still sore from the previous day's exertions, were causing her to cry out in agony.

The leak seemed to be getting worse every minute. She could only paddle a minute or two before having to stop and bail. Then the wind completely disappeared. There was nothing to blow the smoke away, so it blanketed the lake in layers that grew steadily thicker. By the time Emily reached what she thought was the middle of the lake it was no longer possible to see either shore. She wasn't even positive she was still going in the right direction. Her arms were rubbery, the water level inside the canoe was halfway up her calves, and even if she'd still had enough energy to bail there was no way she could keep ahead of the leak.

Emily sat morosely on the wooden seat and watched the inside of the boat steadily fill up with water. The poodle scrambled onto the pile of life jackets and barked angrily. He seemed to blame Emily for the fact he was getting wet again.

Exhausted, Emily felt her earlier sense of optimism evaporate. There was no way she'd be able to finish the journey in the canoe. It was heading slowly but surely toward the bottom of the lake. Even if there'd been one person to bail steadily, and another to do nothing but paddle, the leak was too bad to overcome. Two-thirds of the vessel was now underwater and it was too heavy to paddle. It looked like water would soon start pouring in over the sides.

Emily was reluctant to leave the canoe until she had some idea of which direction to head. She looked around forlornly, seeing nothing but smoke. Then Buttons stuck his head over the bow of the canoe and stared into the general direction where Emily thought the far shore might be.

"Is that the way to land? Maybe you can smell something that I can't see." She sighed. "There's no point in staying in the canoe. My bum is getting wet anyway."

Emily cut off a short piece of her rope and tied the cooler to the life jackets. She carefully lifted the makeshift raft out of the canoe, picked up the poodle, and slowly leaned over until the boat tipped onto its side and she slid into the lake.

The cool water once again brought temporary relief to her throbbing muscles and various burns, although she knew that wouldn't last. Experience had taught her that, before long, the water would start sucking the last reserves of energy and warmth from her body.

The life jacket was designed to keep a person's head out of the water, even if they were unconscious. Experience had taught Emily that the easiest way to swim in one was to lie on her back and kick. She held the poodle to her chest with one hand, grabbed onto the raft with the other, and hoped she was headed in the right direction. There was a real risk of going around in circles.

"Can you die from hypothermia in a heat wave?" asked Emily. "I now believe it is possible. I nearly froze last night. I read somewhere that freezing to death is peaceful, but it sure didn't feel that way to me. I would have given anything for dry clothes and a blanket."

Every once in a while Buttons would raise his head, stare into the distance, sniff, and bark. Emily would immediately adjust her course to head in that direction. She had no idea if the dog knew where shore was, but she hoped that Buttons was being guided by instincts and senses that humans lacked.

She didn't want to ask her sore and weary body to do more than it could, so Emily tried to pace herself. She would kick thirty times and then take a break, counting slowly to sixty. Buttons became increasingly fidgety and it was getting harder to hold onto him. After a while the poodle's teeth started chattering. Emily couldn't tell if it was because of fear or the cold water. She patted the dog's head and talked soothingly in hopes of calming him down. Then, totally unexpectedly and with astonishing speed, the dog launched himself into the lake.

"Buttons!"

Emily turned onto her stomach and saw Buttons splashing through shallow water.

Eighteen

They'd made it to land, although a more desolate and uninviting stretch of shoreline would be hard to imagine. The lake bottom was gooey mud, which Emily knew from experience was very hard to walk on. She decided to swim across it instead, lying flat on her stomach and using her hands to push herself to shore. Buttons was sitting on a large, flat rock. It seemed like as good a place to land as any, so Emily followed the poodle's tracks through the muck.

After pulling herself out the mud flats and onto the rock Emily sat for several minutes and pondered her next move. The fire had burned right up to the shoreline and turned a lush forest into a black wasteland. The ground was littered with smoldering tree trunks. A large stump glowed red hot. It had been turned into charcoal. Walking along the shoreline wasn't an attractive option because most of it was nasty-looking marsh and Emily didn't have any shoes. Cutting through the forest didn't look any easier. Judging from the plumes of smoke she could see rising from the forest floor, there were still lots of hot spots.

Emily felt as if she were trapped on her rock. Despondent, she pulled the raft of life jackets onto shore. She was starting to feel that bringing it along had been a waste of time and energy. She opened the cooler and took out her clothes. Once again the container had proven its usefulness. Everything inside was perfectly dry.

She waited long enough for her underwear to mostly dry before putting on her clothes. Her injured foot still throbbed, although it was no longer bleeding. She couldn't reach clean water, and washing it in the mud seemed pointless, so she simply covered the cut with the biggest Band-Aid she had left. It made her feel a little better, even though it wasn't likely to stay in place for very long, once she started walking across burned ground in bare feet. Buttons stayed beside her on the rock, although he constantly cocked his head and listened intently. Emily hoped the dog wasn't hearing something dangerous, such as another bear. She cut off the dog's primitive life jacket, which was obviously starting to annoy him.

Emily looked through her meagre possessions, wondering if there was anything she no longer needed. In the end she decided to take everything. It seemed doubtful she'd need emergency candles again, but she wasn't prepared to take the risk. She decided she'd continue to wear a life jacket. It might provide some protection from sparks if the wind picked up again. The bright orange colour could also make it easier for rescuers to spot her. There was no doubt in her mind that search parties would soon start looking for survivors, if they weren't already.

She opened up the package containing the blue tarp, wondering how to make use of it. It was made out of thick plastic. As she played with the tarp an idea popped into her head.

"Yes!" she shouted. "I think this could solve my biggest problem."

Buttons stared into the distance, distracted.

Emily read the label of the package the tarp had come in. It was made of something called polyethylene. It certainly felt durable. Excited, she took the knife and used it to cut out pieces of tarp that were roughly the same shape, and just a little bigger, than her feet. Then she cut out a series of long, thin strips.

She stepped onto the foot-shaped pieces and used the thin strips to tie them onto her feet. Before long her feet looked like they belonged to a blue mummy. It wasn't pretty, but her feet now had some protection. As long as she walked carefully, and avoided hot spots, she figured her wrapped feet might take her to safety.

"Hopefully the road to the recreation site runs right along the lake," said Emily. "If it does we probably won't have to walk too far to find it." Having some foot protection had caused her spirits to rise.

With the poodle under one arm and the cooler balanced on her shoulder, she stepped gingerly off the rock and into the dismal remains of the forest. Every time she set her foot down it made a crunching sound and stirred up a small cloud of ash. The polyethylene wasn't thick enough to provide protective padding. She certainly felt every rock she stepped on. Still, it was better than walking through the apocalyptic wasteland in bare feet.

After walking for several minutes Emily came across something very disturbing. At first she wasn't sure what it was. Then she recognized the badly burned carcass of a young buck. It may have been the same deer that had shown her the way to safety the previous day. It was terrible to think the animal had almost made it to the lake, and possible safety, when the smoke and flames brought it down. It occurred to her that birds and animals of many species, especially the very young, would have perished in the inferno. She stood over the deer for a moment, thinking of what her own body might look like if she hadn't escaped.

Emily was very careful about where she stepped and progress was slow. Buttons was extremely restless, complicating the task of carrying him. The poodle clearly wanted to be put down, but Emily could occasionally feel the hot forest floor through the primitive footwear and knew the dog's sensitive paws would be badly damaged if he accidentally stepped on some coals.

Finally, after walking further than she'd originally thought she'd have to, she stepped out from between two huge blackened trunks and onto a dirt road. "We found it!" she cried, causing the poodle to start squirming again.

Emily ran a hand over the surface of the gravel roadway. It was cool to the touch. Except for some brush and grass along the sides there had been nothing for the fire to burn. As the angry camper had said to his wife back at Beaver Creek, "The road is made of dirt and dirt doesn't burn." The road promised the safest route out of the forest. It was rocky, and walking on it with poorly protected feet would be a challenge, but at least there didn't appear to be any danger of stepping on a hot spot.

Emily tied a piece of rope to Buttons' collar and put him on the ground. It seemed unlikely the dog would try to run away, but there was no point in taking chances.

"Which way should we go?"

Buttons yanked on the rope.

"I'm not sure why you want to go toward the boat launch," said Emily crossly. "That's where the access road ends. If we go there we'll have to find the path that leads to the campground and it may still be hot. I think we should go in the other direction, where the guys in the SUV were headed. I'm guessing the road leads straight to a highway. I'd rather walk on a road than a path."

Buttons barked and pulled hard. He hadn't changed his mind about which direction to go. Emily started pulling on the rope but the dog dug his paws into the dirt. Exasperated, Emily gave up.

"Well, when we were in the lake you did seem to know where the shore was. Maybe you're right about this too. If we do find the boat launch we'll know for sure the campground isn't far away. There probably won't be much left, and I don't think there will be any people around, but your guess is as good as mine, maybe better."

Something was troubling the poodle. He would pull on the rope, then suddenly stop and cock his head, listening for something. Then he'd bark frantically for a few seconds. It seemed to Emily that the dog instinctively realized they were headed toward the campground where he'd been separated from his beloved owners.

"Hopefully we'll get you there soon," said Emily.

Although the road was easy to follow it was extremely rocky, making it hard to walk on with sore feet. Emily was very careful where she put every step, which slowed her progress.

Nineteen

There was something strange on the road ahead. Emily stood and stared for a moment, trying to figure out what it was. Then she realized it was a windshield reflecting one of the brief rays of sunlight that occasionally burst through the smoke. She'd found the vehicle that had sped away from the boat launch during the fire, leaving her behind to face the flames. Emily had heard a crash, but assumed it was just the boat flying off the trailer. Now she could see the accident was far worse than she'd imagined.

The SUV had gone off the road, rolled down an embankment, and landed on its roof. Emily knew enough about vehicles to recognize the chrome letters on the front grill. The Range Rover was now a burned-out wreck. An empty boat trailer lay near the rear of the vehicle. It had been ripped off the hitch by the impact.

A short distance away was the fishing boat. It had flown off the trailer and landed upside down, partly blocking the road. An outboard motor lay on the ground a few metres away.

Emily was filled with horror. She'd heard the voices of two men. There may have been other people inside the vehicle, terrified women or children waiting for the men to finish their argument and get out of there. It now seemed obvious that the men had taken too long to pack up. They'd driven right into the firestorm and crashed the vehicle. The end must have been terrible.

As she stared at the SUV it dawned on her that the driver's and front passenger doors were both open. Perhaps everyone inside had managed to escape, just as she had. There was only one way to find out for sure.

The last thing on earth Emily wanted to do was look inside the vehicle. Seeing the dead deer had been bad enough. Just the thought of seeing badly burned human bodies was enough to make her gag.

"I have to do this," she whispered. "The only way to know for sure if there's somebody inside is to look."

Trembling, holding tightly onto Buttons, she slid down the embankment on her backside. Then she got on her knees and peered inside the vehicle. The interior was a complete mess. The smell was terrible. All the upholstery was gone. There were springs, metal frames, and other assorted pieces of metal that flames couldn't consume. But there were no bodies. Emily sat down, fought waves of nausea, and wearily climbed back up the embankment. She was glad there wasn't a charred corpse inside the vehicle. Then it occurred to her that nobody would look forward to finding her body either, no matter how she'd died. A person hanging from a tree or washed up on shore probably looked pretty gross.

"I wanted to be in that SUV," she said to Buttons. "When it took off without me I thought I was a goner. Now I'm glad I was left behind. It would have been awful to be inside the Range Rover when it rolled."

The dog wasn't paying any attention to her. His head was cocked to one side, and he appeared to be listening intently for something.

"You found me just after the SUV took off. Then we went into the lake together. I guess that was actually the safest thing to do. Anyway, we've made it this far." Emily managed a weak smile as she gave Buttons a gentle pat. "Do you believe in fate?"

Buttons began barking and for a moment it seemed to Emily that he was answering her question. Then it occurred to her that he might be calling to someone.

"Nobody can hear you way out here," said Emily firmly. She was about to say more, but something caused her to stop and listen. Was she hearing things, or was that really a human voice? Buttons continued to bark, drowning out all other sounds, so Emily picked up the poodle and tightly held his jaws shut.

There was no sound and Emily had convinced herself that her mind was playing tricks on her. Then she heard it again. A faint cry for help. It came from the direction of the lake. The voice was so weak it was impossible to tell how far away the person was.

Emily let go of the dog's muzzle and Buttons immediately started barking again. His nose pointed straight toward the lake.

"Somebody's in trouble," said Emily. "You're in charge of getting us there."

Twenty

The forest along the road had once been a thick tangle of tree trunks, branches and brush. The fire had turned all the living trees into thin black poles. Emily left the relative safety of the road and slowly worked her way through the ranks of dead trees, always heading toward the faint cries for help. She was already regretting her decision to bring the cooler along. It was heavy and awkward to carry.

She heard the voice again, clearer this time.

"Help! Can you hear me?"

"I can hear you," yelled Emily. "I'm coming!"

Buttons barked and tried to jump out of her arms.

"No!" said Emily, sternly. "I don't want you stepping on a coal and burning your paws." Suddenly she was back on the lakeshore, an unpleasant stretch of muck and rotten logs. Not far from shore, perhaps thirty metres away, was a tiny island with a single sickly tree on it. The island, hardly more than a sand bar, barely rose above the surface of the lake.

Sitting awkwardly on the shore, waving feebly, was a man who appeared to be covered from head-to-toe in mud. He could barely sit up and had to hold himself steady by holding onto the trunk of the tree.

Emily called out. "Are you okay?" She felt silly as soon as she'd said it. Of course the man wasn't okay. That should have been obvious.

"I've got a broken leg, maybe a concussion, and I can hardly breathe," called the man. His voice was hoarse.

"I'm going to swim out," shouted Emily.

She tied the dog to a large piece of driftwood and crawled through the mud on her knees until the water was deep enough for swimming. It only took her a couple of minutes to reach the man. His sanctuary was nothing more than a dangerously unstable mud bank. Emily didn't even attempt to pull herself onto the island. It wasn't big enough for both of them. Besides, the mud was so squishy the man seemed to be in danger of being swallowed up by it.

The man's face, like the rest of his body, was caked in layers of brown sludge that made it impossible to tell how old he was, although Emily had the impression he was middle-aged.

"Are you by yourself?" asked the man. He peered anxiously at the shore, clearly hoping to see a more impressive rescue party step out of the forest.

"It's just me," said Emily. "Well, me and Buttons. The two of us barely escaped the fire. Now we're trying to get back to the Beaver Creek Campground."

"I know the campground you're talking about," said the man, his voice cracking. "It isn't far from here. You should be able to make it."

"What about you? Are you able to walk?"

He shook his head. "My leg is broken." Emily could see that his right foot was pointing in an awkward direction. "I'm in awful pain. There are burns on my face, my neck, and my hands. I've plastered mud on the burns. It helps a little, but I keep fainting. I'm afraid I'm going to drown in the muck. It's like quicksand."

He sounded like he was at the end of his rope.

"I'm Emily Morrisseau. What's your name?"

"Matt Kaloti. I'm so glad to see you. I've heard your dog barking for what seems like hours. I've been yelling, but my voice is weak and I wasn't sure if you could hear me."

"I didn't hear you, but Buttons did."

Matt peered at the shore, where Buttons was pacing restlessly. "It's just a miniature poodle."

"Yes, but he's really smart. He's saved our butts more than once."

Unable to sit up any longer Matt let go of the tree and lay on his back in the mud. Emily was concerned by how quickly he sank into it. He wasn't exaggerating when he said he was worried about drowning in the muck.

"Were you in the SUV that went down the embankment?" asked Emily.

Matt started crying "Yes. My father was with me. I don't know if he escaped. When we went off the road the Range Rover landed on its roof. The air bags deployed. It was like getting punched in the face. I must have passed out for a minute. When I woke up the passenger side door was open and dad had disappeared. We were surrounded by fire. I managed to open my door and get outside." His voice was so low it was barely audible. "I couldn't see dad anywhere. I knew where the lake was, so I ran in that direction. The fire was really intense and I tried to protect my face with my hands, so I couldn't really see where I was going." Matt reached out, touched his injured leg, and gasped in pain. "I stepped in a hole near the lakeshore. That's when I broke my leg. I was barely able to crawl to the lake. Then I started swimming and made it to here."

"It was far enough from shore to keep you safe."

"Barely. The heat was so intense that I thought the water around me would start to boil. That might have just been my imagination. And I had a lot of trouble breathing. I guess the fire was sucking up all the oxygen." Matt raised his head and coughed. "I have no idea if my father is dead or alive."

"I looked inside your car. I'm pretty sure he wasn't there." Emily couldn't be sure the fire hadn't completely destroyed the body, but it seemed unlikely. Enough had remained of the deer to tell what it had been.

"Did you search the area around the Range Rover?'

Emily shook her head. "No. I'd just finished looking inside when Buttons heard you calling."

Matt was once again sinking into the mud, apparently too worn out to keep his head free of the goo. Emily took off her life jacket and put it under Matt's head. "That should keep you from sinking any further," she said.

Matt thanked her weakly.

"We have to get you to shore. Can you swim that far?"

"No. I can barely move."

Emily thought for a moment. "I think I know how to do this. I came across the lake this morning with a whole bunch of life jackets. I tied them together to make a raft. I'll go back to where I left them. You can crawl on top of them and I'll pull you to shore."

Matt nodded his approval of the plan and then whispered, "Emily, thank you for helping me."

"Don't thank me just yet. I usually mess things up."

"I feel safe in your hands." The words, said with total sincerity, caused her to blush.

Matt got up on an elbow and looked carefully at her. "You've got a bad burn on your face."

"I can only see out of one eye right now."

"Please be careful."

"I will."

The shore wasn't very far from the mud bank and Emily was positive she could make it, even without a life jacket. She rolled into the water and swam confidently to where Buttons was waiting.

Twenty-One

Emily spent a couple of minutes tightening and adjusting the strips of tarp that protected her feet. Some were badly frayed and she wasn't certain how much longer they'd hold up. Then, leaving the cooler on the shore, she picked up the poodle and headed back toward the access road. She'd decided it would probably be easier and safer to follow the road than try and work her way along the swampy shoreline.

Retracing her trail through the blackened tree trunks was easy. Every step she'd taken earlier was clearly visible in the thick ash that covered the forest floor. Before long she was back on the road, passing the wreckage of Matt's SUV. It reminded her of how much trouble he was in and prompted her to walk faster.

Emily was limping badly by the time she reached the place where she'd come ashore and abandoned the life jackets. They were exactly as she'd left them, lying in a pile on the shore.

"I'm going to have to trust you to stay close to me," said Emily. Buttons was much calmer than when he'd first heard Matt calling for help. "My arms will be full of life jackets and I can't carry you at the same time."

The poodle seemed perfectly content to be put down and showed no sign of wanting to run off.

Back on the road, feet throbbing, Emily once again had to pass the ruined Range Rover. She went by slowly, checking both sides of the road for any sign of Matt's father. There was nothing. It was certainly possible he'd survived. Emily had. So had Matt. She hoped the older man had also made it as far as the lake and found sanctuary.

When she came to the overturned boat Emily sat on it for a couple of minutes to give her throbbing feet a break. Buttons sniffed at the skiff, whimpered, and then sat at Emily's feet. Something was upsetting him. Emily decided the poodle was worn out and desperate to find his family. She remembered that she still had a small amount of beef jerky in her pocket. The dog seemed to perk up at the sight of the dried meat. He ate the jerky greedily and begged for more.

"Sorry. You got the last of it. I didn't even save anything for myself. Not that I want any food right now. My guts are so messed up from drinking bad water that I'm afraid to put anything else in my stomach." She got wearily to her feet. "I'm sure Matt is wondering where we are."

She walked over the stony ground as fast as her battered feet would allow, followed closely by the poodle, and reached the lake. Matt saw them and waved feebly.

Emily opened the cooler, took out the knife, and cut one of the life jackets free from the primitive raft so that she could wear it. This time she didn't bother tying up the dog. Emily put on her life jacket and pulled the others behind her as she went back into the water. Buttons watched intently, but didn't attempt to follow.

"I got the life preservers," said Emily, pulling herself onto the mud bank. "I think you should put on the one you've been lying on. Then we can roll you onto the ones I tied together to make a raft. Hopefully I'll be able to pull you to land." She waved vaguely at the shore. "It's really muddy there. I'm not sure what we're going to do when we get there. I can't carry you."

"I can't walk, but I should be able to crawl onto shore."

Emily glanced at Matt's feet. "You only have one shoe left."

"The one on my good leg seems to have disappeared. I have no idea what happened." He stared. "What on earth are you wearing on your feet?"

"I lost my hiking boots. I suppose they're on the bottom of the lake right now. I found a pair of flip-flops at a cabin, but they came off when the canoe overturned. They're probably floating around somewhere." She held up a foot so Matt could see the bright blue plastic. "I had to cut up a tarp and use the strips to wrap my feet."

Matt frowned. "They don't look very sturdy."

"They aren't. They don't provide much protection from rocks or . . . or anything really. But they are better than nothing. I've got a gash on the bottom of one foot and it is really slowing me down. If you had two shoes I'd borrow them for the hike to the campground."

Matt struggled to put on his life jacket. "Were you at the campground when the fire hit?"

Emily saw Matt was having trouble so she reached over to help. "Yes. The fire came out of nowhere. It was wild. People were really scared. Everybody headed for an iron bridge where we were supposed to wait for rescue." Emily glanced toward the shore, where Buttons was sitting in the mud. His white fur had been turned an ugly grey by all the ash and mud. "Buttons panicked and ran away. His owners were really upset, so I ran after him and got cut off by the fire."

Matt whistled weakly. "You risked your life to save a dog?"

"Yeah, I guess so." She paused and shook her head. "And I don't even like yappy little mutts."

"You are a remarkably brave young woman," said Matt. "Buttons may not appreciate everything you've done for him, but I'm sure his owners will."

Once again his praise made Emily feel uncomfortable. "Well, he turned out to be a lot smarter and tougher than I thought. He woke me up just before the cabin we were sleeping in caught fire. And then he bit a bear on the nose."

Matt had finally managed to fasten the strap on his life jacket. "How did you manage to get away from the fire?"

"Same thing you did after you crashed. Headed for the lake. I got to the boat launch just as you were driving away. I screamed, but you didn't hear me."

To her astonishment Matt began sobbing. "It's all my fault. Dad wanted to come back to shore almost as soon as we were on the water. He swore he could see flames. I told him he was imagining things. When it became obvious there was a forest fire moving toward the boat launch he said the situation had changed and the best place for us would be the middle of the lake. He said it would be safer. I wasn't going to leave my new Range Rover behind so I said we had to go back to shore. Then I insisted we load the boat onto the trailer. He begged me to leave it behind, but I wouldn't. I thought I'd be able to drive out. I was wrong. Now my father is missing."

"I'm so sorry," whispered Emily, taken aback by the man's unabashed grief. She wondered what her own parents were feeling at that moment. They were probably just as frantic as Matt was. A few days earlier the thought of her parents mourning her death had felt oddly empowering. Now it made her feel ashamed.

Her mother had known for a long time that something was bothering Emily. She asked why old childhood friends no longer called or why Emily no longer called them. But she was so wrapped up in the slow collapse of her marriage that she wasn't as perceptive as she'd once been. Her father was no help. Always self-centred, he'd become increasingly distant over the past couple of years and no longer seemed to have much interest in her life.

Twenty-Two

"We should go," said Emily. It came as a surprise to her to discover tears pouring down her cheeks.

Matt must have assumed the tears were for him, although they really weren't. He gave her arm a gentle squeeze. "All I've done is whine and complain and talk about me. How did you escape?"

"When you guys drove away you left behind an oar and a cooler."

Matt glanced toward shore, where Emily had left the cooler.

"I thought that looked familiar," he said.

"It floats really well. I used it and the oar to get across the lake. We found a shack and thought we were safe. Then there was a windstorm and the flames got so high they made a tornado. That's when the fire jumped the lake. We got away in a leaky canoe, but it overturned and we had to spend the night on a tiny island in a swamp. There was a bear on the island. It tried to get at us once, but Buttons scared it off." She sighed, suddenly overcome with exhaustion. "This morning we set off in the canoe, but it filled up with water and we bailed out just before it sank. We swam to shore."

"I could hear you in the canoe," said Matt. "There was some banging, like a paddle hitting the side, and the dog barking. I kept calling out, but you never responded."

"I didn't hear you, but Buttons did. He knew something was wrong and he wanted to help. If it wasn't for him I never would have found you."

Emily looked around. The swollen eye was really bothering her. "I'm not sure where we should head."

Matt waved his hand at a nearby point. "The boat launch is right over there. Do you think you can get us that far?"

Emily nodded, trying to look more confident then she felt.

"The lake bottom is relatively firm there," said Matt. "That will make it easier to get ashore. There's a decent sized parking lot, so we should be able to find a piece of level ground for me to stretch out on. There's also a trail that leads to Beaver Creek Campground. I think it will be easy to find and follow."

"Okay. Let's go." Emily looked at Buttons. The dog was waiting impatiently on the mucky beach. Hopefully he would keep up by walking along the shoreline. The journey would be dirty, but relatively easy for him. By sticking to the shore the dog would also avoid stepping on any hot coals.

Matt gingerly rolled onto the small raft. It looked like the mass of life jackets, combined with the one he was wearing, should provide more than enough buoyancy. He swore. "Sorry. I just twisted my bad leg and it really hurts."

Emily slid into the water, grabbed hold of Matt's life jacket, and started kicking. At first he attempted to help with his one good leg, but something happened that caused him to cry out in pain, so he stopped. Every once in a while Emily turned her head and looked at the shoreline. She was glad to see that Buttons was working his way through the mud and keeping a close eye on them.

"I can't stop shivering," complained Matt.

"Once we get to shore you'll warm up right away," said Emily. "It's another scorcher."

"I don't mean to be such a baby. I know you've gone through just as much as I have. Maybe more."

"I wasn't injured as badly as you are," said Emily. She stopped kicking for a moment and listened carefully. "I don't like the sound of your breathing."

"My lungs hurt. I breathed in a lot of smoke and hot ashes."

It dawned on Emily that Matt might actually be dying. She kicked with as much energy as she could muster, pausing occasionally to catch her breath. One of her legs cramped up, making it impossible to swim in a straight line.

Matt sensed she was in trouble. "How are you doing?"

"Not well," she reluctantly admitted. "I don't have much strength left."

"We're almost there," he croaked. "I can see the place where we launched the boat."

"Can you see Buttons?"

"Yes. He's making better time than we are. He has to stop every few metres to let us catch up."

Emily gritted her teeth, silently vowed to never go into a lake again, and thrashed at the water with increasing fury and less forward progress. She began to wonder if they would ever make it.

Then, amazingly, she heard splashing next to her head. Buttons had decided to swim out and join them. Emily turned onto her side so she could see the shore. It was almost within reach. She gave a few more thunderous kicks, felt sand beneath her feet, and stood up.

She grabbed Matt by the back of his life jacket and pulled him close to shore. He rolled over and began awkwardly pulling himself onto shore with his elbows. Matt stopped suddenly, reached into the water, and pulled out a silver can.

"Beer," he whispered. "My brand."

"There was some beer and ice in the cooler when I found it," said Emily. "I dumped it all on the ground. I wanted to use the cooler as a flotation device."

Matt held onto the can tightly as he crawled onto dry land.

Emily took off her life jacket, desperate to rid herself of as much wet clothing as was decent. She was astonished to see that a heavy, wooden picnic table had survived the fire. It stood alone in an open area, which had undoubtedly saved it. She limped over to the table and had a closer look. There were some scorch marks and the surface was covered with ash, but the table was as solid as the day it was built. She used her wet life jacket to wipe off most of the ash and went back to the beach.

Twenty-Three

To her surprise Matt had opened the can of beer and was guzzling it. "Are you sure you should be drinking that?" she asked. Emily didn't know anything about beer, except that her mother thought that her father drank far too much of it.

"All I've had to drink in the last twenty-four hours is lake water that tastes like mud and smoke," said Matt. "It's disgusting, and I think it is making me sick. This beer is much safer to drink."

Emily, who had also been forced to drink filthy water, sympathized. Her guts were still rumbling from the sludge she'd consumed in the swamp.

"I see another can," said Matt, pointing. "Would you mind getting it for me?"

Emily walked to the water's edge and fished out another can of beer, which she handed to Matt. "There's a big picnic table just over there. For some reason it didn't get burned. It's a good place for you to lie down. The top is nice and warm to the touch. It will help you get those shivers under control."

Matt put an arm over her shoulder and together they awkwardly limped over to the table. He gratefully stretched out across the top. Emily helped him take off his life jacket. She noticed with alarm that his shivering was not getting any better. Even Buttons seemed concerned. He nuzzled Matt's ear.

Emily sat on one of the table's benches and adjusted the strips of tarp on her feet. Some of them were in danger of falling off. The cooler, containing the knife and remaining piece of tarp, was on the shoreline where Emily had gone into the water to rescue Matt. She considered walking back to get the tarp so that she could cut off some more strips and rewrap her feet. The more she thought about it the less she liked the idea. It would take too long to make her way back to the cooler. Besides, she was worried about Matt's health and wanted to find help as soon as possible.

"How are your feet?" asked Matt. He'd opened the second beer.

"Not good. I'm glad the campground isn't very far away. Hopefully something survived. It would be nice if the van we came in hasn't been destroyed. Maybe Big John or one of the kids left a cell phone behind." She thought for a moment. "I don't suppose you have a phone."

Matt shook his head sadly. "Not working. I checked. I carry my cell phone on my belt. It didn't survive the lake. Good luck finding a signal around here anyway."

"I think I can see the path to the campground from here," said Emily. "I'm going to head off now, while I've still got the strength."

Matt closed his eyes and silently moved his lips. At first Emily thought he was praying, but he was just finding it difficult to speak.

"Emily, I know you're exhausted, and I'm grateful for everything you've done so far, but I'm asking you to do me a huge favour."

"What's that?" There was an edge to Emily's voice that even caught her by surprise. She wasn't in the mood to go wandering through the shallows looking for more beer, which is what she thought he was going to ask.

His voice was so weak she had to lean close to hear the words. "Could you please take a few minutes to look for my father? It would kill me if I discovered he was close by, injured and calling for help like I was."

Emily instantly felt shame at assuming Matt only wanted her to search for beer, but she was also irritated by the request. She had no idea where Matt's father might be. Nor did she particularly want to find his body, if he was dead. The sight of the dead deer had unnerved her.

"I don't know where to look," she protested.

"Please. Just take a quick look in the area around the car. I know it's a lot to ask."

"All right," she said, slowly getting to her feet. It was possible the missing man was still alive, desperately hoping for rescue. "What is your father's name?"

"Sam."

"What is he wearing?" Emily reasoned that if she knew the colour of Sam's clothes it might help her locate him.

The question seemed to puzzle Matt. She wondered if his brain was fuzzy because of all the physical and mental turmoil. "He had jeans and a T-shirt."

"What colour?"

Matt took a while to answer. "I don't remember."

Emily knew she shouldn't be surprised. She'd noticed that men often didn't pay any attention to what other people were wearing.

"I'm pretty sure he had denim jeans and a black top," said Matt slowly. Then he brightened. "He was also wearing a new pair of orange running shoes. I remember making fun of them."

"Orange is good," said Emily. "They will really stick out."

Emily slowly hobbled down the road toward the burned out Range Rover. Buttons followed, upset to be moving away from the campground. After every few steps Emily would stop and check both sides of the road, calling, "Sam! Sam, can you hear me?"

All the vegetation that might normally conceal a body in a forest was gone. The bushes and grass had all been consumed by the flames. Tall, thick trees had been turned into thin, black sticks. There was nowhere to hide. Emily could see a long distance into the charred wilderness.

As she shuffled along the road it dawned on her that the only sounds in the entire forest were her footsteps. There were no singing birds, buzzing insects, or chirping squirrels. It seemed that every living creature had either fled or perished.

After walking for several minutes Emily came to where a culvert ran under the road. She looked at it thoughtfully. She doubted that even a skinny girl like her could squeeze into it, but a desperate man might pull himself into it and get stuck.

"Sam, can you hear me?" she called.

There was no answer.

She slowly picked her way down into the ditch, crying out in pain when she accidentally stepped on a sharp rock. After reaching the culvert she took a deep breath, mustered her courage, and looked in. She could clearly see daylight at the other end of the culvert. There was nothing inside.

Relieved, she got back onto the road and wobbled toward the Range Rover. She'd already decided that was as far as she was willing to go. She'd travelled the section of road that lay past the wreck several times already. If Sam were lying nearby she felt she surely would have seen him.

After reaching the pile of melted plastic and metal that had once been a vehicle she searched both sides of the road. There was no sign of him. Perhaps Sam had managed to reach the lake after all. He may have drowned, or perhaps he was safe on the far shore.

Exhausted, Emily once again sat down on the overturned fishing boat. She fiddled with the strips of tarp that covered her feet, tightening and re-arranging them. Many were wearing thin and wouldn't last much longer. She again thought about going back to where she'd found Matt. The cooler, along with the knife and tarp, were still there on the muddy beach. The remaining chunk of tarp could be used to rewrap her feet.

"Better get going," she said, standing up. Buttons ignored her. The dog was pawing at the road and trying to get his nose under the overturned boat.

Emily watched the poodle for a moment and then gasped in horror. Her brain was racing. She leaped to her feet, grabbed a handle at the back of the skiff, and lifted.

The boat rolled over, landed with a crash, and rocked back and forth on its bottom.

"Crap!"

Sam was lying on his side, an expression of absolute terror on his face. Emily stared at him, unable to look away. How did he get under the boat?

Emily noticed he was wearing black jeans and a blue top, the exact opposite of what his son had thought. However, Matt had been right about the bright orange running shoes.

"Sam, can you hear me?" Her voice trembled. There was no response. Emily knew for certain the man was dead. Buttons sniffed the man's face and whimpered quietly. The poodle seemed to understand that Sam was gone.

All thoughts of looking for the cooler were forgotten. Emily immediately headed back toward the boat launch. She'd kept her promise to Matt. Now she had to tell him what she'd found.

Twenty-Four

When Emily got back to the picnic table she thought she might have another dead man on her hands. Matt was lying motionless where she'd left him. He didn't appear to be breathing.

"Matt! Are you okay?"

She gave his shoulder a squeeze and his eyes fluttered open.

"Emily, did you find my father?" He could barely get the words out.

There was no easy way to tell him. "I'm so sorry." She could barely look at his face. "He didn't make it."

Huge tears left trails on Matt's muddy cheeks. He struggled to sit up.

"Where did you find him?"

"Under the boat. After the crash he managed to get out of the SUV. There was probably fire all around. Maybe he couldn't see a way out and hoped the boat would protect him from the flames."

"Are you sure it's him?"

For a moment Emily was taken aback by the question. Who else could it be? Then she realized she was dealing with a man who was in shock.

"It has to be him. He's wearing orange shoes, just like you described."

Matt's body was wracked with sobs. His lungs sounded like they were about to explode. Emily put her arms around him, partly to offer comfort and partly to keep him from falling off the table.

"I'm so sorry," she whispered. She was so tired and overcome with emotion that she could barely stay on her feet.

"It's my fault," cried Matt. "If I'd done what my father wanted and stayed in the boat he'd be alive today." It took several minutes before he could compose himself enough to say, "He had a bad heart. That's probably what killed him. Hiding under the boat might have kept him safe from the fire, but the stress would have been too much."

Matt held onto Emily for a long time, crying and cursing himself. Finally he let go and collapsed onto the tabletop. "Thank you for finding him," he said. "I know this has been hard on you. You've been my guardian angel. When we get out of here I want to meet your parents so that I can tell them what a special girl they've raised."

She wiped away some tears. "Oh, I'm nothing special. I think that's been well established."

Matt shook his head. "No, you are a very rare combination of courage and empathy."

Emily smiled sadly. "I don't think I'm very brave, but I have always tried to help others." She didn't say what she was thinking, that being kind and helpful wasn't enough. Other kids seemed to interpret it as weakness.

She stood up, nearly fainted from a head rush, and had to hold onto the picnic table to keep from falling. Her last reserves of energy were nearly gone.

"I'd better get going to the campground," she said. "Hopefully there's somebody there. If not I'll hike to the highway. Maybe they've opened it, or maybe there will be fire trucks going by."

As she took a couple of tentative steps Matt watched with concern. "Are you going to be able to make it?"

"I hope so."

"You can barely walk."

"My feet are really sore. The plastic wrap helped a little, but it's falling apart."

Matt frowned. "You can't walk through a burnt forest in bare feet. You should take my father's shoes. He has average-size feet for a man. You're tall so I'm guessing your feet are bigger than average for a woman. I'll bet his shoes fit you. Even if they are a bit too big they'll be better than walking across hot ground with rags around your feet."

Emily froze. The first thing that came to mind when she saw the orange shoes was that they looked like they'd fit. Then she'd thought about actually taking the shoes off a dead man and was repulsed by the idea.

"I don't think I could do that," she said in a low voice.

"I know dad would want you to."

"I don't feel comfortable taking them off his feet."

"If you won't do it, I will." Matt struggled to sit up.

Alarmed at how weak he looked, Emily put her hands on his shoulders and gently pushed him back into a prone position. "The boat is too far away. You'll never make it."

Matt sounded determined. "You need to have shoes. If you won't take them off Dad's feet I'll get them myself. Even if I have to crawl."

Just the idea of touching a body made Emily anxious. The thought of taking the shoes off a dead person and putting them on her own feet sent shivers down her spine. Matt studied her face and seemed to understand what was going through her mind.

"Have you ever inherited something that belonged to someone else?" he asked. "Someone who is now dead?"

"My grandmother left me her pearls."

"Have you ever worn them?"

"Yes. Just to try them on and see how they look."

"Did it feel wrong when you put them on and looked in the mirror?"

She thought for a moment. "No."

Matt reached out and took her hand. "Right now those shoes are far more valuable, and much more important, than your grandmother's necklace. Those shoes could save our lives."

He was right and Emily knew it. Her feet were already so tender it seemed unlikely she could go much further without proper shoes. Matt needed medical attention. The simple act of breathing was painful to him.

"Okay, I'll do it," she said.

Once again she got up and started limping toward the boat. Buttons watched, clearly perplexed by what was going on. It seemed to Emily that her companion was desperate to leave that desolate place. Buttons whimpered as he watched her move off, but elected to stay with Matt. The little dog was worn out.

As she shuffled along the stony ground Emily came to the conclusion that Matt was absolutely correct. She stood little chance of making it to Beaver Creek campground without some sort of footwear. Every step was torture.

The tarp strips did not protect her toes, and at least two of them were bleeding.

As Emily walked she formed a plan. She decided the only way she'd have the courage to take the shoes was to do it as soon as she arrived. If she hesitated, even for a moment and thought about it, it was likely she'd loose her nerve.

When she rounded a corner in the road and saw Sam she briefly stopped and looked away. She remembered the tortured look on his face and didn't want to see it again. After taking a deep breath she moved forward, keeping her eyes on the shoes.

Emily knelt on the ground and tugged at the first shoe. It came off immediately, which was a huge relief. The second didn't come off as easily. She tugged several times, felt a rising sense of panic, steeled herself, and then untied the laces. The shoe came off.

With a shoe in each hand she walked over to the boat and sat on one of the aluminum benches. The first thing she had to do was take off the polyethylene strips. Some fell away with the slightest tug, but others were still tied firmly together. Emily had to pick apart a number of tight knots before all the ribbons tumbled to the ground.

The shoes were a little too big, but not so large that they were awkward to walk in. She took a few steps and revelled in the sensation of being able to walk over rocky ground without suffering excruciating pain.

"Thanks, Sam," she whispered and once again set off for the boat launch.

When she got back to the picnic table Matt moved his head so he could see her feet. He smiled. He was barely

135

able to speak, but still tried to make a joke. "Ugly colour and, knowing Dad, they were the cheapest shoes on the shelf. Still, they should get you to the campground."

"I'm going to head off now," said Emily. "Is there anything I can do for you before I go?"

Matt shook his head and closed his eyes. He seemed to be fading fast. Emily looked around for Buttons. The poodle had gone to the lake for a drink. Emily considered doing the same thing, and then remembered the water along the shoreline was muddy.

"I'm going, Buttons," called Emily. "Are you coming with me or staying with Matt?" The poodle sat listlessly on the ground. He watched with sad, exhausted eyes.

Emily glanced at her watch. It had finally stopped working, after being immersed for the fourth time in two days, but she guessed it was early afternoon. She walked to where she thought the path came out of the forest and quickly found it. The fire hadn't affected the hard-beaten earth, although parts of it were covered in nearly ankle-deep ash. It looked like the trail was going to be easy to follow.

Glad to have some good fortune for a change, Emily set off. Although her feet were bloody and sore, Sam's shoes protected them and she was able to walk at almost a normal pace. To Emily's surprise Buttons, who seemed to have found renewed strength, joined her. The dog appeared to understand they were finally moving toward the campground where he'd last seen his owners.

The path was wide and the hard-packed ground had cooled off. Emily felt her spirits rise, even though she wasn't sure how far it was to the campground. When she'd tried to catch Buttons during the evacuation, and then run through the forest to escape the fire, she had no idea the path even existed. She hadn't stumbled onto it until just before she'd reached the lake.

Emily noticed that Buttons was limping badly. She knelt down and inspected the poodle's paws. One of the pads had a discoloured spot that looked like it might be a burn.

"No more walking for you," said Emily, scooping the dog up in her arms. "I'm going to carry you home. Luckily I don't think we have too much further to go."

Buttons seemed grateful to be picked up and rested his head on Emily's shoulder.

"I wonder what we're going to find at the campground? Maybe there are people around, or maybe everything is gone."

Emily was deliberately talking out loud. The silence of the forest once again unnerved her. Everything that had once called it home had fled or perished in the flames. The stench of ashes smelled like death.

It was hard to believe, but the original inferno hadn't completely burned everything. Smoke was still rising from a hundred different places. Stumps and logs smoldered, like campfires abandoned in a hurry.

Emily's throat was raw and dry, partly from the smoke and partly from thirst. She was beginning to regret not drinking from the lake when she'd had the chance. Even muddy water would taste good at that moment.

Twenty-Five

The quiet was shattered by a loud crack. Emily froze, not sure where to turn. Directly in front of her was a large pine tree. Flames had eaten almost all the way through the base of the trunk. The pine slowly toppled over and then crashed into a row of smaller black sticks, the remnants of what had once been a grove of young trees. The sound of crashing trunks and splintering wood echoed through the dead forest. Just moments earlier the trail ahead offered clear and easy passage. Now the path was blocked by a tangled mass of blackened branches and trunks. A sinister-looking cloud of ash rose high into the sky.

It dawned on Emily that if she had been walking just a little faster the falling trees might have hit her. On the other hand, if she'd left the boat launch a couple of minutes earlier, she would be well past the danger zone and walking on a clear path.

Now she had to find a way around the barrier of broken trunks and branches. The detour forced her to leave the relative safety of the trail and walk through deep piles of ash and uneven ground. The grey powder could be hiding hot spots or deep holes. Emily walked slowly, testing the ground with a foot before putting any weight on it. Every step kicked up a small, dirty cloud of ash. Her shoes were soon filthy, but they protected her feet.

When she reached the end of the tangled pile of deadfall Emily sighed in relief. The way back to the path looked clear. Then she heard a familiar and unwelcome crackling sound. The falling trees had exposed a massive knot of roots, some of which were red hot. As soon as they were yanked to the surface and exposed to air some of the roots burst into flames. Emily decided to give the newborn fire a wide berth. Ominously, some of the smoke seemed to follow her as she walked. It caused her good eye to water.

As she picked her way through the desolate wasteland Emily noticed a plume of smoke rising out of a hole in the earth that was no bigger than a quarter. She sensed she was in a dangerous area and was glad to see the path to the campground was dead ahead.

Eyes stinging, eager to reach the path, she moved away from the deadfall and the growing flames. Her route took her close to a smoldering tree trunk. As her right foot touched the ground it broke through the surface and Emily toppled forward. Instinctively she reached out with both hands to break the fall, dropping Buttons. The startled dog landed with a yelp.

Emily's right leg was trapped inside a deep hole. She shrieked in pain and horror. It felt like hot pokers were being pushed into her flesh. Off balance, in a panic, she struggled to pull her leg free. She reached for the nearest tree trunk and saw at the last possible moment that the trunk was speckled with coals that would burn her hands. Next to the trunk was a thin black stick, all that was left of a sapling. Emily grabbed it and pulled with all her strength. As she felt her foot start to come free her weight wrenched the sapling's roots out of the earth. Emily barely got her leg out of the ground before the pole she was holding onto broke in half.

She rolled away from the hole, yelled in pain, and grabbed her leg. Two holes had been burned through her pant leg. She couldn't tell how bad the burns were, just that they hurt. Then she noticed her shoe was gone. It had come off when she'd pulled her foot out of the hole.

The prospect of trying to walk out of the fire zone with one bare foot was horrifying. Emily carefully crawled on her belly to the hole. She peered down and saw a tangle of roots and small flames. Her shoe was at the bottom. She reached in as far as she could, brushed against the shoe with a fingertip, felt a lace, and pulled. To her profound relief the shoe came out of the earth. There were several scorch marks on it, but it had not been badly damaged. She gave it a shake, just in case there were hot coals inside, and put it on. It was only then she realized the dog had disappeared.

"Buttons!" There was no response.

She wondered if he'd been hurt when she stepped into the hole and dropped him. It would be a disaster if he was injured and lost in the ruined forest. Fighting through the pain of the new burns she tried to follow his trail through the thick ashes, frantically calling his name.

To her profound relief the poodle stuck his head up from behind a rock and barked.

"Come here, Buttons."

The dog obeyed, limping badly. Emily picked him up and held him tight. "I don't think I'll be able to go on much longer," she said. "We'd better make it to that campground soon." The exhausted dog didn't make a sound.

As soon as she was back on the path Emily picked up the pace, trying to ignore the jolts of pain that shot through her right leg with every step. The combination of smoke, painful burns, and stress made her eyes water, making it even harder to see where she was going.

Twenty-Six

"We made it," whispered Emily, hardly daring to believe.

She was standing at the edge of the Beaver Creek Campground. There wasn't much left. Emily limped onwards, passing burned-out vehicles and melted camping gear. After a couple of minutes she reached the ruins of a cinderblock building. The walls had survived, but the roof was gone. It was still possible to read a sign that marked the entrance to the women's washrooms. Water dripped from an outdoor tap. Buttons started licking the spout, reminding Emily of how parched she was.

To her surprise and delight the water system was still working. When Emily turned on the tap a steady stream of cool and clear water poured out. She put her head next to the spout and drank deeply. Then she caught water in her cupped hands for the poodle to drink.

When Buttons had drunk his full she splashed water on her filthy and burned face. It brought almost instant relief. Then Emily took off her jeans so she could see how bad her new injuries were. There were two burns on her calf and one on her ankle. The largest wound was about the size of a bottle cap. They were extremely painful.

She washed her feet and legs and walked gingerly to a plastic lawn chair that had somehow survived the fire. Someone had left a beach towel on the chair. Emily shook off the ashes and saw the towel was undamaged. Rolling around on the forest floor had left her jeans covered in soot. There were also numerous holes and scorch marks on the right leg. She didn't want to put the filthy and tattered jeans back on, so she simply wrapped the towel around her waist.

Somewhat rejuvenated Emily set off in search of Big Jim's van. If it still existed she could retrieve her bag, get clean clothes, and maybe find a cell phone to call for help.

It was a very large campground and the section she was walking through had been the most heavily forested. Emily could tell the fire had been intense. Every vehicle, tent, and RV she walked past had been badly damaged or destroyed.

Then she came across an SUV that was still intact. Oddly, it looked like a vandal had poured red paint over it. The vehicle, including the windows, was now almost completely crimson, although you could still see splotches of the original colour.

Puzzled, Emily stopped for a moment. Then it dawned on her what the red stuff really was. She'd seen television news clips about forest fires. The stories often featured video of large planes dropping clouds of a red chemical on fires to put them out. She thought she might have heard it described as fire retardant.

She tried the door of the SUV, in case something useful had been left behind, but it was locked, so she walked on. Buttons had also been revived by the water break. He was still limping, although not as badly, and didn't ask to be picked up. The small dog was more alert than he had been in hours.

Emily now reached a part of the campground where most of the vehicles and camping equipment had survived the fire, although there were still a few scattered burned-out wrecks. Almost everything that hadn't been destroyed was covered in retardant.

As she walked slowly through the campground, unsure of exactly where she was and where Big Jim's van was parked, Emily realized that visibility was gradually improving. The smoke was finally lifting.

While passing a large van that had apparently been abandoned in the middle of the road Emily noticed that one window had been left open a crack. She peered inside and hooted in delight. A cell phone had been left on the passenger seat.

She wasn't an expert on cell phones, but was pretty sure that she didn't need a passcode to make an emergency call. Emily figured that if she got the phone she should be able to call 911, assuming there was cell service in the area.

The opening at the top of the window was almost, but not quite, wide enough for her put a hand through. She struggled for a few minutes before frustration got the better of her. At one time she simply would have given up and walked on. That was before she'd watched a log cabin filled with valuable supplies go up in flames. She'd played that night over in her mind countless times and realized she should have broken into the cabin.

Emily looked around for a moment and saw exactly what she was looking for. She picked up a baseball-sized rock from a fire pit and threw it as hard as she could. The window dissolved into thousands of tiny pieces. She reached inside, opened the door, and grabbed the phone. It was dead. She opened the glove compartment, hoping to find a charge cord. No luck.

Emily felt a wave of regret at breaking the window. If there'd been pen and paper she would have left a note. Since there was no writing material she simply put the phone back and hoped insurance would pay for the broken window.

Minutes later she saw the entrance to the campsite. The sign welcoming visitors to Beaver Creek Campground still stood, although nothing remained of the registration building except for its foundations. Not far away, in the empty field they'd had to pretend was a campsite, was the charred hulk of Big Jim's van. It was in an area that hadn't been hit by the airborne retardant.

Emily walked morosely to the van. At first she couldn't figure out why it had been destroyed. There was nothing flammable nearby. The field was mostly hard-packed dirt with small clumps of grass. Then it dawned on her that some of the windows had been left open when Jim and the other campers had fled. It was possible sparks had blown into the vehicle and set the contents alight. Everything inside the van was gone, including any cell phones that might have accidentally been left behind.

She was staring at a charred piece of fabric that had once been her backpack, cursing her luck, when she realized Buttons wasn't there. The dog had been obediently following her through the campsite and had shown no inclination of wanting to wander off.

More puzzled than alarmed, Emily looked around. Not seeing the dog she called his name. An answering bark came back immediately. Buttons sat in front of a motorhome that was coated in red retardant. He looked at Emily expectantly and barked again.

"You made it home!" Emily called, delighted. "That's the motorhome that belongs to your mom and dad."

At first she couldn't remember their names. Then it came to her. Eric and Anne Rossi. Buttons hadn't been fooled by the change in the motorhome's colour. He knew exactly who it belonged to.

The euphoria of reaching the campground and finding fresh water for drinking and bathing had largely worn off. Emily was once again feeling the effects of the past day and a half. She could still only see properly through one eye, every muscle in her body was aching, and her new burns hurt terribly.

Buttons started barking desperately, obviously keen to get inside the RV as quickly as possible.

"I've already broken into a boathouse and a vehicle," said Emily, hoping the sound of her voice would help calm the poodle down. "Hopefully I don't have to break into the motorhome as well. Your owners seem like very nice people and I don't want to damage their property."

Emily ran awkwardly toward the motorhome, conscious that she was becoming lightheaded and wobbly on her feet. She was out of breath when she arrived and had to grab at the door handle for support. To her relief the door wasn't locked. She opened it and Buttons immediately scurried up the metal steps and went inside. Emily followed, unsteadily, a few seconds later.

Twenty-Seven

Most of the windows were covered with retardant, so there wasn't a lot of light inside the motorhome. Emily noticed a light switch near the door, touched it, and a nearby wall lamp came on. The RV's batteries were still good.

Buttons sat on the floor, staring intently at a cupboard. When Emily didn't pick up on the clue right away the dog whined and sat on his haunches, demanding food. Emily got the message, opened the cupboard, and found a stack of canned dog food.

There was a small but well-equipped kitchen area near the door. Emily opened a drawer that looked like a logical place to put utensils and discovered that her guess was correct. She quickly found a can opener. Buttons barked excitedly.

Emily began opening cupboards, looking for a dish to put the dog food in. She saw a stack of soup bowls and decided one of them would work just fine. Buttons was famished and attacked the food when it was put in front of him.

Watching the poodle eat reminded Emily that she'd hardly eaten anything in nearly two days. She took a can of fruit salad from the same cupboard where she'd found the dog food, opened it, took a fork out of the cutlery drawer, and ate out of the can.

She looked through all the cupboards and discovered that Eric and Anne didn't believe in travelling light. They had enough canned food to last for weeks. The couple also had a fondness for snacks. Emily opened a large bag of potato chips, a calorie-heavy treat she usually avoided.

After checking all the cupboards and storage compartments Emily opened the fridge. It was no longer cool, indicating the power to it had been turned off. There were some packaged luncheon meats, which Emily wasn't about to risk, and a wide variety of canned drinks. The cans were no longer cold to the touch, but their contents would be safe to drink. Emily selected an iced tea; it tasted simply amazing to her. After draining it she took a second. She sat at the RV's dining table, which was large enough for four people.

Buttons had licked his dish clean and jumped onto the neatly made bed at the rear of the vehicle.

"It looks like you're usually allowed up there," said Emily. "But they may change that rule when they see the mess you're making." There was hardly any white fur visible on the dog. Because of all the soot and mud his colour ranged from light grey to black. Astonishingly, there was still a pink bow on one bedraggled ear.

Emily picked up the dog's dish, put it in the small sink, and froze. In front of her, attached to the wall, was a first aid kit. How had she missed it earlier?

She unsnapped the kit from its wall mount and carried it to the table. The Rossi's kit proved to be very well stocked, unlike the one she'd found at the shack on the far side of the lake. There was a wide variety of bandages, a bottle of extra strength ibuprofen, antiseptic towels, and even packets of burn cream.

It seemed unlikely that over-the-counter pain medication was going to be strong enough to relieve her throbbing wounds, but it was better than nothing and she swallowed a couple of tablets. Then she cleaned her cuts with antiseptic, applied the burn cream, and put bandages over various burns and cuts.

The combination of food, drink, and painkillers had a strange effect on Emily. At first she felt a huge energy burst. Then she became lightheaded and found it difficult to concentrate. To make matters worse her stomach cramps returned. An emergency visit to the RV's tiny washroom left her feeling miserable. Her legs were so rubbery that she was hardly able to make it to a bench in the dining booth. Even after laying her head on the table for a few minutes she was barely able to concentrate again.

Emily wondered if emergency crews had already searched the campground, looking inside every vehicle and motorhome as soon as it had been safe to do so. If so, she understood they'd probably been looking for her.

Emily figured that other people would be anxiously waiting for the highway to reopen so they could return to the campground and recover whatever vehicles and camping gear that had survived the fire. She had no idea how long it would take for the first visitors to arrive. It may be just a matter of hours or it may take a day or two.

It wouldn't matter much either way, if all she had to worry about was herself and Buttons.

The motorhome offered a safe, comfortable space to wait for help. It contained a large supply of food and drink. Emily was pretty sure her wounds, while extremely painful, weren't life threatening. Buttons was exhausted and had a sore paw, but otherwise he appeared to be in good health.

Unfortunately, Matt wasn't so lucky. His injuries were serious. She worried that if he didn't get medical attention soon he might die. There was no way he could be left by himself on the picnic table for a day or two. Every minute he spent alone was probably agony.

As she thought about Matt she began to feel guilty about the time she'd spent in the motorhome. Then she realized that she might be allowed to cut herself a little slack. There was no doubt she'd been in dire need of food, water and first aid when she'd arrived at the ruined campground. Emily still felt woozy whenever she stood up.

Rescuers could still be a long way off, or they might be around the next corner. She wouldn't know until she started hiking. At least there would be no more stumbling along rocky paths and squeezing between smoldering tree trunks. To the best of her recollection the road leading into the campground wasn't very long. Less than a kilometre. Then she'd be at the highway with its smooth asphalt, easy walking, and the possibility of being found by a passing motorist.

"I've wasted enough time," she said vehemently. Buttons didn't even look up from his bed. "We have to get going." The sleeping dog trembled and whimpered as if he were having bad dreams. "I guess I have to get going as soon as I figure out what to do with you." Emily stood over the poodle and worried what she should do next. Buttons was worn out. He was also lame, meaning Emily would have to carry him if she took him along when she hiked out.

Buttons started to snore, making Emily smile. "Get a good rest, little buddy," she whispered. "You deserve it. You saved my butt. Matt's too."

Emily was thinking about leaving Buttons in the RV. It was a comfortable and familiar space to him. However, she knew it was wrong to leave an animal in a locked vehicle, especially in hot weather.

She considered the dilemma, took another look around the motorhome, and came up with up with a possible solution. The door and several windows were equipped with screens. She opened a sliding glass window and felt a slight breeze come through the screen. Emily thought that if she opened everything with a screen the interior of the RV wouldn't overheat.

There was lots of canned dog food, so she could open several cans and put them on the floor beside a large bowl of water. If Buttons had to go to the bathroom, too bad for the people who would have to clean it up. Emily suspected the dog's owners wouldn't mind too much.

She found two heavy bowls in a cupboard and decided to fill both of them with water. That way Buttons wouldn't go thirsty if he accidentally tipped one over.

There was snack food and bottled drinks inside almost every cupboard, so Emily knew she wouldn't have worry about hunger or dehydration during the hike. What she did need was something to carry the supplies. When she stood up, planning to search the motorhome for a bag or container, she nearly fell over. Her legs were so wobbly that she had to hold onto the table for support. After a few moments she felt steady enough on her feet to resume the search.

Almost instantly she saw exactly what she was looking for. There was a large beach bag next to the driver's seat. She took a quick peek inside and saw a towel, some romance novels, and sunscreen. She dumped the bag's contents onto the passenger seat, confident she now had something large and durable enough to carry food and water. She held the bag upside down and gave it a final shake. A set of keys fell out. Keys for the motorhome.

Emily was delighted with her discovery. "Good news, Buttons!" The dog reluctantly opened an eye. "I don't have to leave you behind, after all," she said, voice shaking. "I've already done a couple of B&E's, knocked down a door with an axe, and used a rock to smash a car window. Stealing a vehicle shouldn't be a big deal for a badass like me."

She picked up the keys.

Twenty-Eight

E mily realized there were some huge advantages to driving instead of walking. It would take her less time to drive to the nearest town than it would take her to limp a few hundred metres. Time was important. Matt needed help as quickly as possible and Emily suspected she was too weak to hike very far. She couldn't even stand up without feeling light headed.

Although the driving idea was very attractive, she could also see a potential flaw in it. The problem was that Emily only had a vague idea of how to drive. Many of the kids she went to school with were preoccupied with getting their driver's licence. Some, boys especially, could hardly talk about anything else. Many of them bragged they'd already done a little driving with a parent on a country road or empty parking lot. One girl, who was notoriously rich and spoiled, had taken her father's Corvette without permission and rear-ended a police car. Emily wasn't surprised when the car thief, already queen of the mean girls, saw her status among all the other cool kids rise even higher.

Emily had never been particularly interested in learning how to drive, although she'd always planned to eventually get her licence. She rarely watched what her parents did when they were driving, preferring to daydream or watch the scenery.

One thing she did know is that vehicles come with an owner's manual. Her mother sometimes referred to hers when she needed clarification on something, such as how to reset the clock or find out why a red light had suddenly appeared on the dashboard display. Emily understood that the traditional place to keep these booklets is in the glove compartment.

The compartment was right where she expected it to be, between the driver's and front passenger seats. Inside was a jumbled pile of maps, novels, sunglasses, and energy bars. At the very bottom was the owner's manual. She opened it and started reading.

Starting the vehicle seemed easy enough. Emily had seen her parents do it scores of times, even if she hadn't really been paying attention. She tentatively adjusted the driver's seat, which looked and felt like an expensive recliner. First she determined that her feet could reach the gas and brake pedals. The next thing was to find out which was which. The manual provided the answer.

"Gas on the right. Brake on the left," she read aloud, a habit she had developed while studying. "And where I'm sitting is called the cockpit."

Then she found the illustration that identified the various gears. Park and neutral seemed very much alike. She decided drive and reverse were probably the important ones, since they controlled whether the vehicle was going forward or backward.

Because the interior lights were working Emily suspected the RV's batteries were strong and the engine would also start, but there was only one way to find out for certain.

She took a deep breath, put the key into the ignition, and turned. The dashboard display immediately came on. The engine turned over, but didn't stay on. Puzzled, she leaned over the steering wheel and tried again. Her foot accidentally touched the gas pedal as she turned the key and the engine started purring. "Give the engine some gas when trying to start it," she muttered. "Must remember that."

Her next problem was the windshield. Most of it was covered in fire retardant. Only a small section on the driver's side was clean, making it difficult to see the road.

Emily thought it would be relatively easy to wash the rust-coloured chemicals off the windshield. It wasn't. After going outside, spraying the windshield with water and rubbing with a dishtowel, she realized she was just smearing the dye and making the problem worse. Emily decided there was no time to look for another way of cleaning off the fire retardant. She was already feeling guilty about the length of time she'd stayed at the campground. There was a small bit of windshield, no larger than the cover of an average paperback book, she could look through. It wasn't much, but it would have to do. There was a slightly larger section of clean glass on the passenger side window, allowing her to see the edge of the road.

Eric Rossi had expertly backed his motorhome into the campsite. The front of the vehicle was pointing directly at the campground access road. That was a piece of luck.

Emily didn't fancy the idea of trying to back up the big vehicle.

As she was about to climb back into the motorhome it occurred to her that the bottom step was very close to the ground. The steps might be damaged if the RV went over a bump. Emily fiddled with them for a moment and discovered they easily folded up.

With a growing sense of dread, Emily got into the driver's seat, peered through the clean patch of windshield, and put the vehicle into drive. Not knowing any better she floored the gas pedal and screamed aloud when the motorhome jumped forward like a rabbit. There was a loud metallic clang from outside. She slammed on the brakes and the vehicle came to an abrupt stop. When she took her foot off the brake the motorhome started moving forward again, although much more gently.

"Park!" she yelled, nearly overcome with anxiety. "Put the stupid thing in park." She shifted to park, wondered briefly if it should be in neutral instead, and then went outside to see what she'd run over.

The loud bang had been caused by a pair of folding lawn chairs that had been left leaning against the back bumper. They'd hit the ground when the RV moved forward. Nothing had been damaged. Relieved, she went back inside.

"I've been wasting too much time," she said through gritted teeth.

She took a deep breath and put the vehicle into gear. Even without her foot on the gas it moved slowly, but smoothly, forward. Steering it was surprisingly easy, and although her heart was racing, Emily had no difficulty getting out of the campsite. She tentatively put her foot on the gas and gently pressed down. The vehicle immediately picked up speed, causing her to gasp. A quick glance at the vehicle's head-up display showed she was only going ten kilometres an hour.

Trembling and sweating she steered the vehicle onto the access road and out of the campground. It was a narrow lane, barely wide enough to allow two vehicles to pass each other. Both sides of the dirt road had been heavily treed and one of the burned trunks had toppled across the road during the fire.

Emily, who was having a lot of trouble seeing through the windshield, noticed the log at the last moment and immediately slammed on the brakes. Once again the vehicle came to an uncomfortably fast stop.

From inside the motorhome Emily couldn't tell how significant the obstacle was. Deciding to inspect it up close, she put the vehicle in neutral and went outside.

The tree had been tall, but not much thicker than one of her legs. The branches were all gone, leaving just a black trunk behind. She decided the RV could go over the log without much difficulty. The question was whether it would be better to go over it slowly or to go as quickly as possible.

Emily turned to get back into the motorhome and was startled to see that it was rolling backwards and picking up speed. She yelped in alarm and raced after it. There was a slight curve in the road and the vehicle was veering toward the remnants of a very large tree. Running as fast as she could she climbed through the door, nearly stumbling in the process, ran to the cockpit, and just as a rear wheel went off the road, hit the brakes.

"There's a reason they call it park," she yelled, furious at herself. "When you park a vehicle, put it in PARK. That should be obvious."

Emily didn't even want to see how close she'd come to getting the motorhome stuck or damaged. She slowly drove forward, reached the log, and gunned it. The vehicle easily went over the obstacle, but she nearly flew right out of the seat.

"Probably should have taken that a little slower."

Emily looked to the back of the vehicle to see how Buttons was doing. The jolt from going over the log had awakened the poodle, and he looked at Emily with concern.

"Don't worry," she told Buttons. "I'll take it slower the rest of the way."

The dog whimpered, apparently unconvinced.

A pungent haze still hung over the burnt landscape, red chemicals covered most of the windshield, and because Emily had vision in just one eye she could hardly see where she was driving. She stayed in the middle of the lane and tried to control a rising sense of panic.

She nearly ran into another fallen tree. It was much larger than the first one. There was no way Emily could go around or over it. She stopped the vehicle, put it in park, and got out to have a closer look.

The first thing she noticed was that the highway was only a few metres away. She'd almost accomplished one of her main goals. The highway was wide and smooth. Once on it she knew she could drive all the way to Vancouver. There were lots of towns and farms before then, and it seemed likely the nearest people were only a few kilometres away.

Matt's suffering had to be brought to an end and that meant she had to get onto the highway. The only thing standing in her way was the tree. The trunk had snapped in half when it hit the ground. She wondered if that might work to her advantage. Emily gingerly touched the tree to see if it was hot. It wasn't, so she grabbed the trunk and pulled. It hardly budged. She wasn't strong enough to move it on her own.

Emily glanced back at the motorhome. It had just occurred to her that maybe she could use the powerful vehicle to pull the tree out of the way. The front bumper was flush to the vehicle, preventing her from tying her rope to it. She checked the back end and discovered there was a trailer hitch. It was the perfect place to tie her rope. Now all she had to do was turn the vehicle around so she could tie the trunk to the hitch.

The road wasn't wide, so there was very little room to manoeuvre. Emily remembered that her father could turn his pickup truck around in tight spaces by repeatedly backing up and then driving forward for short distances. Although Emily wasn't sure she could pull it off she decided she had to try, for Matt's sake.

She put the vehicle in reverse and turned the steering wheel. Then something wonderful happened. The RV had a back-up camera, and as soon as the vehicle was put in reverse a dashboard monitor came on. She could see exactly where she was going. The camera was a priceless tool and Emily felt a huge sense of relief.

She drove backwards a few metres, turned the steering wheel, drove forward, and then repeated the process. In less time than she'd thought possible the vehicle's back end pointed directly at the tree. Emily took out the rope tied one end to the trailer hitch and the other to the shorter section of trunk.

Back behind the steering wheel Emily gently pressed down on the gas pedal, unsure how much power was required to move the tree. The engine revved, but the motorhome didn't move. She gave it more gas and the vehicle slowly started to move forward. The sound of something heavy being dragged across a rough surface could be heard over the sound of the engine. The tree didn't have to be moved very far, so Emily only drove for a few seconds. Her plan had worked. The top section of the tree had been pulled free. Half the road was now open. It looked wide enough to drive the RV through. She untied the rope and put it back in the fanny pack, just in case it was needed again.

Turning the motorhome around again went a little smoother and faster the second time. When she successfully squeezed past the larger section of tree trunk she exhaled in relief and whispered, "I'm sorry this has taken so long, Matt. Hopefully things will go better now."

Twenty-Nine

Emily paused at the highway. Should she turn left or right? She knew Big Jim had driven past some tiny communities and homesteads on the way to the campground. That was probably the logical way to go. For all she knew there was nothing but bush if she turned to her right. She turned left. The cockpit display informed her that she was heading west and had nearly a full tank of gas.

She quickly discovered that by following the highway's centre line she could stay right in the middle of the road, which made her feel more comfortable. Luckily there was no oncoming traffic. As her confidence rose, so did her speed. In a matter of minutes she had travelled farther than she would have been able to walk in a whole day.

As she drove the smoke began to thin out. There was even an occasional glimpse of sky. The forest on both sides of the road had been completely destroyed. She passed the smoking ruins of what had once been a farm. Only the foundations remained of a house, barn, and several smaller buildings. Emily hoped everyone, including the animals, had escaped.

She kept an anxious eye on the speedometre. Trial and error convinced her that the fastest she felt comfortable at was about twenty kilometres an hour. She knew it was ridiculously slow for a highway, but she didn't want to risk an accident by going faster. So far she hadn't even put a scratch on Eric's RV. Knowing that made her feel proud.

It occurred to her that the motorhome had a radio. She was starved for news about the fire. Uncertain of where the radio controls were, and not wanting to take her eyes off the painted line, Emily decided to pull over and take another look at the owner's manual.

She gently touched the brakes and was pleased to see the motorhome responded by gradually slowing down. Parking in the middle of the highway seemed unnecessarily risky. At some point the road would have to be reopened. Perhaps it had been already. A big truck might come barrelling down the road at any moment.

Looking for a safe spot to pull over she put her face close to the windshield and peered through the clear section of glass. She was astonished to see a ditch filled with green vegetation. None of the grass, weeds, and brush had been burned. Trembling with excitement, she put the vehicle in park. She moved to the passenger side seat, looked out the side window, and discovered that she'd reached the boundary of the fire zone.

Buttons could tell the motorhome had stopped. He jumped out of his bed and sat in front of the door.

"I'll bet you need a bathroom break," said Emily. She stood up, felt woozy, held onto the back of the seat to steady herself, and then walked slowly to the door. As soon as the door opened Buttons jumped gingerly to the ground. One of his paws was obviously still sore.

By coincidence Emily had parked the RV right where the fire had been stopped. When she looked to the right there was nothing but devastation, but on her left there was green pasture and a red barn.

A horse stood in the pasture, looking at something in the blackened brush. The animal did not appear to be injured or perturbed. Then Emily noticed something that caused her to gasp out loud. Parked close to the barn were two pickup trucks. They were crew cabs, dark green in colour. They were close enough that Emily could identify the BC Forest Service logos on the doors. Where were the firefighters? Emily couldn't see anybody. Then she noticed that the horse was staring at a nearby thicket. She wondered if the horse knew something that she didn't.

Moments later a man wearing a red shirt and yellow helmet came out from behind the brush. He was carrying something that looked like a long-handled spade. The man stopped and poked at the ground with the tool. A second firefighter appeared. The two men spoke briefly and then one of them pointed toward a thin plume of smoke rising from a stump in the burned area.

"Hello!" called Emily. Her voice was too weak to carry far. The firefighters didn't hear her. For a moment Emily thought of walking over to where the men were working. There was a barbed wire fence between her and the firefighters and she realized she didn't have the strength to climb over it. Her legs were wobbly and she still felt faint. She called again, but the men still didn't hear her. Their attention was focused on a small group of firefighters working their way through the blackened trunks.

Emily decided to go back to the cockpit and lean on the horn, but Buttons acted first. He'd seen or heard the firefighters and started barking furiously. The firefighters heard him, looked up, and saw Emily standing in the doorway of an RV that was covered in fire retardant and parked in the middle of the highway. They immediately dropped their tools and ran toward her. They were young and fit and reached the motorhome quickly.

"Are you okay?" asked the first to arrive. He had a slight French accent.

"Yes, I'm fine," she said. Then she fainted and toppled out of the door, face first, toward the pavement. The firefighters caught her before she hit the ground. They carried her inside the motorhome and put her down on the bed. When she came to, a different firefighter was splashing water on her face and Buttons was licking her hand.

The newcomer was middle-aged and had an air of authority. His face was black from soot and smoke. Bright blue eyes looked at her with concern.

All the rest of the crew crowded into the motorhome. Emily noticed that one was a woman. She was as filthy as all the rest.

"Is your name Emily?"

"Yes."

The crew cheered.

"I'm Jacob," said the older man. "Everybody has been worried sick about you."

"A fire service first aid attendant will be here shortly," said the woman. "I'm going to call for an ambulance. We need to get paramedics here right away."

"You've got some nasty burns and bruises," said Jacob.

"There's a man who needs help more than I do," said Emily, struggling to sit up. "His name is Matt Kaloti. He's

164

got a broken leg and can hardly breathe. I think his life is in danger."

"Where is he?" asked Jacob, his tone urgent.

"He's lying on a picnic table at the Hawkeye Lake boat launch."

"I know exactly where she's talking about," said one of the firefighters. He started talking into a radio, giving instructions.

"Matt is on our list of missing people," said Jacob. "So is his father."

"Sam Kaloti is dead," replied Emily. She started to cry. "He died in the fire. He's lying in the middle of the access road, near an aluminum boat and burned-out vehicle."

More information and instructions were relayed by radio.

A vehicle door slammed. Someone else had arrived. It was the fire crew's first aid attendant. He shooed all the other firefighters, with the exception of Jacob, out of the motorhome.

The new arrival was one of the tallest and skinniest men Emily had ever seen. He looked like an ungainly bird, but he was gentle and seemed to know what he was doing. After a fast but thorough examination he said, "You're going to be okay, although I'm sure those burns are painful. You'll definitely want to have that eye checked out by a doctor. Provincial paramedics are on their way. They'll take you to hospital in an ambulance."

In the background a voice said, "First responders are on their way to the boat launch."

"What happened?" asked Jacob. "How did you get separated from everyone else when the campground was being evacuated?"

Emily reached over and gave the poodle a pat. "This stupid mutt ran off in a panic. His owners were frantic. I thought I could catch him and bring him back. I was wrong. I had no idea a forest fire could spread that quickly." The dog panted gently, looking pleased with himself. Emily squinted and smiled. "I can't believe that pink ribbon is still holding on."

"So you risked your life to save a dog," said the first aid attendant, who was doing something to one of the burns on her calf.

"Yeah, but he paid me back with interest. He woke me up and warned me the fire had jumped the lake. Then he chased off a bear that was trying to get at me. And it was Buttons who found Matt when he was barely alive and clinging to a mud bank." She winced as the first aid attendant touched a particularly sensitive area. "I have to say that my opinion of miniature poodles has gone up considerably."

"How did you escape the fire?" asked Jacob.

"We swam across the lake. There weren't a lot of other choices. We found an unlocked cabin on the other side, so we went into it. When the fire jumped the lake I got away in a leaky canoe, but it was too hard to paddle in the windstorm. Then we were nearly hit by a falling tree."

"We call those widow makers," said Jacob.

"Anyway, the canoe flipped over. That actually worked out okay because I discovered you could hide underneath it and still breathe. We spent the night in a swamp, which is where Buttons bit the bear, and this morning we crossed the lake again. The canoe sank, so we had to swim to shore. That's when we found Matt." She frowned and leaned back. "I'm sure there's more to the story, but my head is pretty fuzzy right now."

"I understand you were on a survival course," said Jacob. "What sort of gear did you have?"

Emily closed her eyes and was quiet for a moment. "The clothes I was wearing." She reached into the fanny pack and took out the rope. "And this."

"That's all! Just some rope?"

"The rope was very useful," she said. "I probably wouldn't be alive without it." To the surprise of the two men she burst into laughter. She now knew, beyond any doubt, that she didn't want to die.

Jacob, a man who appeared to be used to working with rope, neatly coiled Emily's cord together. "You did remarkably well."

"I'll say," said the first aid attendant. "I can't imagine how anyone could have done better."

"You actually survived a Rank 6 fire," said Jacob, shaking his head in astonishment. "That means you can survive anything life throws at you."

A voice outside yelled, "They found the guy at the boat launch. He's still alive. The smoke has cleared enough to get him out by helicopter."

Emily smiled. "I kept my promise to you Matt," she whispered so softly the two men could barely hear her.

"Would you like something to drink?" asked Jacob.

Emily licked her cracked and bleeding lips. "Yes, please."

"We've got some ice-cold water in the truck."

"That would be great."

Jacob went outside where the rest of the crew was waiting. They'd obviously decided fire mop-up could wait for at least a few more minutes.

Emily heard the man with a French accent ask, "How is she doing?"

"She's going to be okay. You won't believe everything that's happened to her. That girl is one tough cookie."

"Did she have any survival gear?"

"Just this rope. She gave it to me. Says she doesn't want to use it any more. I'm not sure what she meant by that."

There was the sound of running footsteps. The female firefighter came barging through the doorway and handed Emily a cell phone. "Your mother is on the line." Emily took the phone. She could hear her mother sobbing.

"Hi, mom."

"Emily! Are you okay?"

"I'll be fine." Emily was surprised at how weak her voice was.

"You don't sound like you're fine."

"My brain is pretty fuzzy, especially when I try to stand up. And I've got a few burns. Nothing serious, but they really hurt. I might end up with a couple of interesting scars."

Her mother took a deep breath. Emily knew she was trying to compose herself. "Is it true you ran into the fire to save a dog?"

Emily sighed. She was in no mood for a lecture. "I know it was a stupid thing to do. All I can say is that we made a good team, and I wouldn't have made it without him." She suddenly felt nauseous and nearly threw up.

Her mother could hear that something was wrong. "Emily?"

168

"Sorry. I'm having trouble keeping things down. Listen, about the dog. His name is Buttons. This morning he led me to a man who was hurt during the fire and couldn't move. If we hadn't found that man he might be dead by now."

"I'm glad you found him."

"And I think I found myself."

There was a long silence. "What do you mean?"

"We'll talk about it when I get home. Okay?"

"Okay." Her mother broke into a fresh spasm of sobs. Emily knew from experience that this could go on for some time unless her mother had something else to think about. "Mom, I want you to promise that you'll never try to make me go camping again."

"I promise."

Something was happening outside. It sounded like another vehicle had arrived. Emily heard a woman's voice say, "Is she in the RV? Good. Can she walk or do we need a stretcher?"

"I can hear something in the background. What's going on, Emily?"

"I think they are going to put me in an ambulance and take me to hospital." Emily took a deep breath. It was best to strike while her mother was still emotionally fragile. "Do you think we could get a dog?"

BARRY MCDIVITT worked as a journalist in radio and television for more than thirty years. His previous publications include the Thistledown titles, *Redcoats and Renegades* and *The Youngest Spy*. His stories have appeared regularly on the Global TV network and the CBC radio and TV networks, as well as in a wide variety of newspapers and magazines. He presently writes Young Adult novels and works as a communications director in high-tech. He lives in Kelowna, British Columbia.